runs in the blood

I0891571

runs in the blood

STORIES

MATTHEW J. TRAFFORD

ARSENAL PULP PRESS
VANCOUVER

RUNS IN THE BLOOD
Copyright © 2025 by Matthew J. Trafford

All rights reserved. No part of this book may be reproduced in any part by any means—graphic, electronic, or mechanical—without the prior written permission of the publisher, except by a reviewer, who may use brief excerpts in a review, or in the case of photocopying in Canada, a licence from Access Copyright.

ARSENAL PULP PRESS
Suite 202 – 211 East Georgia St.
Vancouver, BC V6A 1Z6
Canada
arsenalpulp.com

The publisher gratefully acknowledges the support of the Canada Council for the Arts and the British Columbia Arts Council for its publishing program and the Government of Canada and the Government of British Columbia (through the Book Publishing Tax Credit Program) for its publishing activities.

Arsenal Pulp Press acknowledges the xʷməθkʷəy̓əm (Musqueam), Sḵwx̱wú7mesh (Squamish), and səlilwətaɬ (Tsleil-Waututh) Nations, custodians of the traditional, ancestral, and unceded territories where our office is located. We pay respect to their histories, traditions, and continuous living cultures and commit to accountability, respectful relations, and friendship.

Arsenal Pulp Press is committed to reducing the consumption of non-renewable resources in the making of our books wherever possible. We make every effort to use materials that support a sustainable future. This book is printed on paper made with 100 percent sustainable recycled fibre content.

This is a work of fiction. Any resemblance of characters to persons either living or deceased is purely coincidental.

The following stories were previously published in different form: "In Our Own Image" in *The Malahat Review* 205, and in *Queer Little Nightmares* (Arsenal Pulp Press, 2022); "This Is How We Remember Kyra" in *Exile* 47.1; "Sixteen Seconds" in *The Ex-Puritan* 37; "The Mine Monster of Britannia Beach" in *Lumina* XVI; "Strike Anywhere" in *The Ex-Puritan* 32; and "Far from the Tree" in *Fables for the 21st Century* (Banff Centre Press, 2018).

Cover and text design by Rebecca Poulin
Cover images by Francis Barlow, *Eagles Screeching at an Owl*, etching, via the Wellcome Collection; and François Perrier, *A Centaur with Cupid*, etching, via rawpixel
Edited by Catharine Chen
Proofread by Alison Strobel

Printed and bound in Canada

Library and Archives Canada Cataloguing in Publication:
Title: Runs in the blood : stories / Matthew J. Trafford.
Names: Trafford, Matthew J., 1979– author
Identifiers: Canadiana (print) 20250145049 | Canadiana (ebook) 20250145111 |
ISBN 9781834050140 (softcover) | ISBN 9781834050157 (EPUB)
Subjects: LCGFT: Short stories.
Classification: LCC PS8639.R34 R86 2025 | DDC C813/.6—dc23

for my daughter, Sophia Peter Elizabeth Lind

Now most of our ill-health comes from two places—the brain and the back. We made two mistakes; one was to stand up and the other was to start thinking. It strains the spine and the nerves. It makes tension and the brain makes the body.

—John Updike, *The Centaur*

CONTENTS

IN OUR OWN IMAGE

"LET'S MAKE A BABY," he'd say sometimes. I'd had lovers say this before, in that callous way tops can have about them: *We haven't been using condoms but we just can't seem to conceive. I've been going in bareback but it's just not working.* We both used condoms, though; we found it more sanitary. I took this phrase to be a little quirk at that time in our relationship when the idiosyncrasies and small flaws were what began to bind us together.

"Let's make a baby, Marcus." I never took him seriously, because I never knew how serious he was about *me*—how could a connection this strong last for very long? That wasn't the way it happened, not for me or for anyone I knew. But when he cried in front of me for the first time, cried *sober*, cried and said he didn't want to be alone, that he was terrified sometimes that I would leave him, then

I finally believed he was mine, and I began to think that maybe he was serious about a child.

Even though this potential child was safely in the future—we didn't even live together—I found out what the paperwork looked like, what we had to prove, whether an insurance underwriter and an actor-slash-sommelier could really afford a baby, and so on. When I mentioned this to him, he reacted badly.

"I don't want to adopt," he spat. "I want us to make one, you and me—a baby that comes from us."

I didn't know what to say, what he meant—what the hell was he talking about? But he seemed so sincere, so defenceless as he said it.

Soon after, he asked to move in, and I was ecstatic—finally my life might be as I had imagined. He would barely make an impact on my carefully decorated condo. I'd been to his place, of course, and he had very few belongings beyond his clothes, like some travelling magician or gap year backpacker. So when he suggested he wanted the spare room, which I barely used, for his study, I figured that was an acceptable compromise. Men and their man caves. It was just an empty little room—an electrical outlet, a sturdy table, and a bench. Maybe he had a hunting rifle from his grandfather he would want to polish from time to time. Maybe he had some hobby that he engaged in once in a while when his life seemed too monotonous or his job too boring. Maybe he wanted to lay down old world reds and liberate them with flair at the dinner parties we would throw together. I could deal with these things. I had read about Bluebeard and his wives, the dangers of curiosity. And so I left him his one little room, the only place I didn't fuss over and clean and have complete anal-retentive control over.

When he did bring in his meagre baggage on the first of the month, there were no surprises. He had his tennis racquet and his workout gear, an inflatable armchair—which I sternly forbade—a lamp, a guitar, some knick-knacks—among them, two polished onyx orbs he jokingly called his "balls"—and an urn that contained the ashes of his beloved childhood dog, Cooper.

We didn't have pets in my house growing up, though I often felt my brothers and sisters were acceptable substitutes. There was this old lady who lived across the street. I thought of her as very old, though probably she wasn't much more than fifty, which doesn't seem so far away to me now. Her husband was seventeen years older, and he'd had a stroke that left his face paralyzed and drooping like melting wax. She parked him on the porch, and he sat there in the shade most of the day. She'd feed him his lunch of baby food, not much different from what my younger siblings ate, and he'd drink through a straw, and he would groan at you with a little spasm of his right arm that my mother told me was meant to be a wave and should be properly answered with a wave in kind and a greeting of, "Hello, Mr. Monahan." I complied with all my mother's instructions at that age, but I always felt a shudder of horror when he jerked at me and moaned. I always tried to cross the street so I could reasonably pretend to be out of earshot when I passed by.

The Monahans also had a dog, which my father called a Dogue de Bordeaux and my mother called a mastiff, who was very old and had severe hip dysplasia—I can say that now, though at the time I thought it was the result of an accident. Maybe the Monahans had dropped him out a window, for that was how he looked: all splayed out. Mrs. Monahan had rigged up a sling for him of her own design. You see these now with wheels attached, but hers was much more low-tech, simply a swath of canvas that scooped up his hind legs, and she would walk him twice every day. If I ever saw her coming home from one of these walks, she would be red faced and puffing, sweating profusely, and as she rounded the corner Mr. Monahan would moan and wave, and the dog would howl, and altogether it was the most embarrassing scene I could imagine. I remember asking my mother why she did it—why she kept Mr. Monahan at home, why she didn't put the dog down. My mother said, "She loves them." Something about the way she said it was so final and so commanding that I didn't ask her anything else. But I thought maybe my mother was a fool.

Things started going wrong on a Sunday, though I didn't know it then. On Sundays, we slept in, made greasy breakfasts to combat our hangovers, and spent the day being domestic and lazy and stupid. He'd read the paper for hours, dozing half the time, and I couldn't even manage to resent him for it because he looked so happy and so much like my father and because he was so unequivocally mine. So I would clean and do the laundry and hate it and love it at the exact same time.

On this particular Sunday I was going through the pockets of his jeans to make sure they were empty before throwing them in the washing machine, and I found a receipt from when we'd gone out for Chinese food a couple nights before. I crumpled it and went to throw it in the garbage, but suddenly he caught my arm in that rigid grip of his.

"I want that," he said. His eyes were on fire. I had thought he was sleeping, unaware of where I was or what I was doing.

"Okay," I said. I felt awkward. "Sorry. For taxes?"

"For our baby," he said. "This is part of who we are."

I kissed him dismissively, because I didn't know what else to do, and went back to sorting laundry. He put the receipt in the pocket of the pants he was wearing, but I wondered where it would end up. Was he making a scrapbook? Would I just be taking it out of another pair of jeans a week later?

There was a thing we liked to do sometimes when my mother would phone. She always picked the worst times, and no matter how innocently the conversation started, I inevitably ended up in tears, feeling criticized and small. He would start kissing my neck while I was still on the phone with her, and he'd slowly undress me as I made my excuses and tried to end the call, which always seemed to take forever. In the end he'd take my underwear off with his teeth just as I was hanging up and we'd go at it like teenage boys. I loved him for it. But a few times—this was after that Sunday with the receipts—I couldn't find my underwear afterward. I assumed they'd been kicked somewhere in the heat of things, but it bothered me not to be able to locate them. He didn't take it seriously and told me to lighten up. I was convinced we would have company over sometime and someone's dog or curious toddler would pull my skivvies out from under a couch, and we would all die of embarrassment. Eventually I gave up looking. It never occurred to me that he was taking them.

I can't explain how it felt when I found it. I think there's always some relief in that kind of a moment: This is it, this is the secret, this is the thing that's wrong with him that allows him to love me, this is what he was hiding, this explains every time I didn't feel totally happy even though I had this man to love me. It doesn't matter what you find—proof of another lover, a secret stash of porn, macabre pictures, strange costumes—once you've found it, something drops into place, a thousand tiny mysteries get solved even as your stomach sinks below your knees and the room begins to spin.

We had tickets to see *Pygmalion* at the Grand, and I couldn't find him. One of my greatest pleasures was seeing him dressed up in formal clothes, sitting beside him in the dark and hearing his confident, booming laugh, feeling his hand on my knee. We were late. We couldn't miss it. And so I popped my head into his special room, a door I had never opened since he'd moved in, and I saw it lying there on the table, about a foot and a half long, staring blankly up at me with the black globes he'd used as eyes. The head looked so large for a baby, the face a bizarre amalgam of the two of us—how did he make it so accurate? The bridge of his nose, the ridge of my brow. For a moment I just marvelled at how good a sculptor he was. I'd had no idea he was capable of something like this.

Its feet were pointing toward me, and I could see inside its body. He'd formed the frame from coat hangers, those ones from the dry cleaners he told me he'd taken back, instead put to this other purpose, like my underwear, like so many lost and forgotten things. The body was stuffed with used condoms, tangled and stuck together like shed snakeskins, hardened with time and whatever we'd left in them. A baby of latex and soiled white cotton. There was hair in there too, I could see it, though my eyes were not so good in the dim room that I could tell which one of us it had come from. My God, had he gone through the garbage digging for this stuff? Had he scraped hairs off the scummy shower soap and wiped them off his fingers into the innards of this disgusting thing?

A hot roil started inside my belly, and a copper taste filled my mouth as I realized the man I loved was so profoundly and completely insane that it was wrong of me not to have noticed. Criminal. Impossible.

And so, there was a choice lying there before me. I could reject the man who cooked for me and warmed my bed at night and snored softly beside me and killed spiders in the sink when I was too scared. I could denounce the man I loved for the lunatic he was, have him committed somewhere, treated, endure the sympathetic stares of friends as we all hoped he would get better, pretended things could still work out, even though we all knew they wouldn't. Or, I could lie to him, pretend not to have discovered this until he forced me to look at it.

And then he stepped out from behind me. He was staring at me, but he looked wrong; he was holding his jaw in a strange position that changed the shape of his face. I realized he was chewing something, his cheeks bulging with the mass of it. Our eyes were locked—I couldn't look away. I'd never seen the expression on his face before. He held his upturned palm in front of his mouth and carefully spat something white and pulpy into his hand. Then, finally, he looked away from me to the thing that he'd made and started stroking it, adding chubbiness to its left arm. This was where the receipts had gone, the newspapers that had never made their way to the recycling bin, the grocery lists and the Post-its I'd left to tell him I loved him, the bits of paper that made up our ordinary lives, chewed and masticated into something he could mold, a saliva-soaked sludge he had pressed as a plaster with his fingers, shaping this thing before me.

I couldn't move. I knew that he would say something eventually. He had to. And I knew that, by what he said, my decision would be made.

"What do you want to call him?" His voice was hushed. It was the gentlest tone he'd ever used with me, and the most terrifying thing he had ever said.

I closed the door and left him to his final ministrations. I knew I should have done something responsible—called his family, maybe, to see if there was a history of mental illness I didn't know about. If maybe he had had this kind of episode before. That thought comforted me, somehow. Maybe as a teenager his parents had caught him creating a bizarre sex doll, maybe he had spent time at a facility that would take him back now and know exactly how to deal with this problem. And then he would return to me, whole again, and we would go on as if this had never happened.

But I knew there was no facility. And I was too scared to call his parents. I'd only met them a handful of times, at big family functions, and we weren't close. I didn't want to upset them, prompt them to come here, do something that could worsen the entire situation. I didn't know if I could make myself say the words to them.

And so I left. I went to Justin's house—we'd slept together once, but that was years ago. I'd always had the sense he wanted to start things up again, but I wasn't interested. I suppose that made us friends. What passes for friends. Anyway, I went there, and I asked for a drink.

"Do you remember ..." I trailed off. He arched his eyebrow at me as he poured honey-coloured whisky into a cut-crystal glass, curious and inviting. "Did I ever tell you about those neighbours I used to have as a kid?"

"Yeah, the really devoted wife? I think about her all the time." He handed me my bourbon, I changed the subject, and we drank. I don't even know how much we drank; I only remember the first four. I woke up on his couch with a terrible headache at 3 a.m., and I left without saying goodbye.

Then I walked all the way home, watching the neon lights give way to the daylight. I was prepared to do something. Grab some clothes, tell him I needed a little solo trip to adjust to my new life as a father—after all, I hadn't had as long as him to get used to the idea. Something like that, just to get me out of the house. It was reasonable. Or maybe I could grab some things and sneak out before he even woke up. It was just before six. But when I got inside, all those thoughts disappeared.

I'll never know how he did it. I missed those first moments because of my night out, and now it was a secret thing between them how he'd made his hideous creation come to life.

At first I thought he was puppeteering—I actually reached out my hand and moved it over and below to see if there were any wires. Then I thought that it must be animatronic, that there were motors inside, little tiny ones that made it move in set ways. I knew he'd spent some time in California right after college, and he never talked much about what he'd done there. Maybe he'd worked in movies, learned props and special effects before moving on to the secrets of the vineyard and coming back home.

But there was something so organic about it, the way its eyes actually found my face, the way they followed me when I moved around the room. It was paper white, vampiric, faint little lines of text like veins beneath the surface of its skin. And the eyes were black, so deeply black. They were stone; they were night.

That was when he asked me, "Do you want to hold him?"

For a moment I imagined myself as some modern-day Medea—I would dash its head against our Italian marble countertop. I would draw a warm bath and gently immerse it, not holding it down to thrash and drown, but letting it slowly dissolve, teasing it tenderly apart until it was only wire and floating latex refuse and mush in our tub. I would set it on fire and launch it off the balcony and let out a scream of victory, knowing all I had done was merciful, ultimately humane.

Then he handed it to me with a pleading, proud look on his face, a kind of smile I'd never seen. It was not warm when I took it. It felt cold and clammy against my arm, a dead fish. My flesh prickled. Instead of cooing or gurgling, it let out a pained, haunted moan. Or else I did. At any rate, I recognized the sound.

Then I said, "Hello."

THIS IS HOW WE REMEMBER KYRA

IMPROBABLY, AWKWARDLY, we have arrived. My breath comes short and fast as I take in the room: this maelstrom of swirling taffeta and tulle, surrounded by smiles lacking both front teeth as sugar-smacked lips peel back in grimaces of delight, a soundscape of shrill screaming so high pitched as to be nearly ultrasonic, such that every dog in the surrounding square mile will surely be tucking its snout beneath its paws and whining in distress. Primary colours twirl by like Easter eggs gone mad; Alice running past instead of the White Rabbit, late for a pinky-swear or a thirst-quenching glass of punch that will be referred to as "drink" and solely by its colour, the only hues brighter than the dresses themselves: purple drink, red drink, orange drink. The floor scattered with more glitter and sequins than a drag bar at last call, tiaras akimbo as these schoolgirls careen across the room, painted like pageant queens, JonBenét Ramsay makeup covering complexions a little too sallow, eyes a little too sunken, with burnished copper, millennial pink, patriarch blue.

This is my daughter's third Kyra O'Neil Memorial Princess Party, but it is my first. Nancy has always brought her before, but she couldn't today because she's finally *getting back to her career* and *feeling like herself again.* Nancy would be all dimples and small talk with this set, she would know exactly how to do it, but all I get are glares. Of course, I don't have the privilege Nancy does—of seeing her features clearly imprinted on Bell's face, for starters. It's been ten minutes and two different people have already asked me if I'm the "other" mom. No, you backwater troglodytes. Nancy is not Bell's mother more than I am just because Bell was inside of her. Just because they share DNA, that little ringlet of nucleotide collusion between the two of them, deep in each and every cell. I have been here for every moment from conception onward, and my role has not been secondary, not an afterthought. I am every bit Bell's mother, as much as Nancy.

Nancy, who said it was my turn. Who said—glibly, I might add—that she was *sure I could do it.* Who thanked me for pulling my weight. That's partnership, that's sharing, and that's utter stinking bullshit. I should not be here.

I, who once had two women on leashes lick my boots at the Dyke March while hundreds of people clapped and cheered; I, who was crowned Ms. Butch two years in a row; I, with my short-cropped hair and my beautiful bulky body and my no-shit attitude, am being forced to endure this twee madness by my six-year-old daughter, who is dressed as the most passive princess of them all, Sleeping Beauty. And all I can think is that this sprawling display of commercialism and misogyny, this paean to heteronormativity and consumerism, this is not why I became a mother.

And yet my heart is breaking because my daughter is crying, and she is crying because, of all the goddamn things, her hair isn't blond enough. The other girls have wigs so that their hair will be the exact Pantone yellow of the princess in question, but my little girl came with her natural hair. And though we paid two hundred dollars—which for me is a whole year of haircuts, I shit you not—to get it crimped and curled into this elaborate coiffure, now she is in tears bordering on hysterics because it's not quite the right shade. Her hair is beautiful, like my wife's, one of those neat tricks of biology to show the world over and over again that Nancy is the one who carried her—the "real" mother, as one particularly insensitive bystander just put it—but I loved watching Nancy's gorgeous doe-coloured hair grow out of our daughter's head, and I brush it with her for hours at a time, and now here she is, bawling, because she isn't the right kind of blond. Not like in the fairy tales. Not flaxen, not yellow as gold.

We never even knew Kyra, not that that's the point, exactly—this event grows bigger and bigger every year and now has three chapters in two different states, as Kyra's mother breathily informed us with her hand over her heart and tears welling onto the Kleenex she was holding precisely in place so as not to disrupt her perfectly applied makeup. I wonder what this woman was like before Kyra passed away, or before she got sick. I think terrible things like that all the time. Like, that maybe Kyra is better off where she is, on some *other side*, or simply gone, but in either case away from these parties and these women.

So why are we here?

It's because Bell had a friend in school—just junior kindergarten, which seems like it shouldn't count, but what to call it if not "school"—a friend named Shauna, and they were inseparable and my heart leapt every time I saw them holding each other's hands and running from one thing to the next, or just screaming into the wind or playing in the leaves. This was maybe through September and October, which for children is a lifetime, and that was when we started saying, "She's so big," or "She's growing up so fast," which we still say and which we will probably keep saying for the rest of our lives. But by Christmas Shauna wasn't coming over anymore, and Bell said that she hadn't been at school for a while, and we just didn't know what to do because we didn't even have her parents' phone numbers, which suddenly seemed like an egregious oversight that kept Nancy up at night. But we had only ever seen them at school pickups or drop-offs or at the park; we hadn't yet got to the phase of sleepovers, though we had been worrying about it because we weren't sure what age was normal to start and we weren't sure what people would think of having their kids stay over with a couple of dykes, not that anyone was ever anything but supportive to our faces, but you just never know what's really going on inside.

And then we got a letter from the school, explaining that Shauna wouldn't be coming back, that she was gravely ill with leukemia and that they were using the word *palliative* to describe her condition. We were encouraged to *explicate* this to our children however we saw fit—like that would be an easy conversation—and to prepare ourselves and our child(ren) for the worst. Which, of course, happened not long after. Nancy and I could never quite figure out how much Bell understood, really understood, about that loss. Or whether she was even capable of understanding its permanence and implications at her age.

And then, as it turned out, another classmate's mother who wasn't coping too well found out about the Kyra O'Neil Memorial Princess Party, an international fundraising organization for little girls with cancer who want to go to Disney World, which was Kyra's dream vacation before she died at the age of six. Everyone in Bell's class just *had* to go, and so here we bloody are.

I couldn't help myself this morning—I printed out pictures of young girls in impoverished countries from the Because I Am a Girl and World Vision websites. A whole stack of profiles of girls in communities in least-developed countries where they merely subsist, in need of the basic necessities of life, clean water, and education. I keep slipping them into the purses of the mothers when they're not looking. It's not that I think rich white girls with cancer don't matter, but do they matter *more*? If everyone here gave what they are planning to give to this stupid charity to an organization that actually helps girls in need around the world, they could save so many more lives, make so much more of an impact. A few minutes ago I literally watched one woman donate six thousand dollars—a grand for each grand birthday party during Kyra's short life—which honestly would more than cover donations to one of my flyer girls for twelve years: forty dollars times twelve times twelve. Twelve years! At that point, the child they were helping would be an adult contributing to her community. And this rich white girl who is displaying complete and utter cultural insensitivity by wearing a Pocahontas costume will be long dead. Will it really matter whether she's been to Disney World or not? I'm sorry, I know it sounds awful, but I really think it's true.

My daughter's name is Bell, and I don't care what your opinions are about that. I know what it's like to have a difficult name, having gone through life with the unfortunate moniker of Hanneke, a name I do not suit at all, but I won't apologize for *Bell.* At least it sounds normal when you hear it. But there are two things that piss me off about how people take her name, and they are the exact reasons why it was so important to call her that. The first mistake, of course, is that they spell it with a terminal *e*. Belle like beautiful, Belle like the princess currently picking her nose and wiping it on a plastic tablecloth. Belle is one of the less popular princesses here today, probably because her simple blue peasant dress doesn't appeal, or because even her princess gown—after the man has taken her into his big lavish house against her will, enslaved her, actually—is too yellow and gaudy and puffed out to convincingly recreate. It's somehow too '90s, despite the Emma Watson remake. Some people are soft on Belle because she's supposed to be the smart one—*She loves reading!*—but it never seemed right to me that the smart one let herself get trapped in that way: sacrificing herself for the mistakes of her father, falling for the bad boy. Not to blame the victim, but come on.

And the second mistake people make all the time, including three people here so far this afternoon, is that they think my daughter is named after the inventor of the telephone, Alexander Graham Bell. As though lesbian mothers would name their daughter after a man.

And then I say, "No, Bell, like bell hooks." And people invariably say, "Who?" Thanks again, you just proved my point.

I have this fantasy of just tearing the whole place up, screaming and turning tables over and stomping around like Godzilla, squishing all these little screaming princesses around me. And not one of these mothers would try to stop me. Because there are no heroines here, no matter how hard they try.

This is not an "interesting look." It's my identity.

These mothers don't know what to make of me. They want to be accepting and nice to me because they know that's what they're supposed to do—being cliquey bullies isn't socially acceptable anymore. I mean, they still do it, but they know they should hide it. So they want to be nice—maybe they can be the one who wrangled the lesbian into the PTA or the tea social or whatever—but they can't help what they feel when they look at me. It's not even the fact that I'm partnered with a woman that bothers them, it's that I have short hair and dumpy taste in clothes and probably weigh as much as two of them put together—and I'm *proud* of it. That's what gets them the most.

I place a pile of flyers beside the punch bowl, girls with acid burns on their faces who have been ostracized by their families staring pleadingly out at the rest of us with their wet, needy eyes. One of the other mothers sees my finger lovingly trace a scar on an inkjet-printed cheek.

"Someone's been putting those everywhere," she clucks. "I even found one inside my purse!"

I make a tittering, outraged sound that I don't recognize. I just hope I'm not blushing. She grabs the flyers and stomps them over to the recycling bin. "These images are just so upsetting," she says. "There's no reason for the girls to be looking at things like this, especially not today."

I nod in mute agreement and fury and wordlessly walk away, wondering if I can fish the flyers out later. I keep wondering what Kyra herself would have thought of this party, of these girls, of their mothers. If she would have wanted her name to be used for this legacy. I think, *This? This is how we remember Kyra?*

I walk to the other side of the room. I look around for Bell with a flicker of panic and then see her, sitting cross-legged with three other girls in the middle of the floor, talking about who knows what, seeming to the world as though they've been best friends their entire lives. Every time I watch her at play it amazes me how kids who are strangers find each other and decide, seemingly at random, to leave each other alone or to be inseparable companions for a few hours, only to be forgotten as soon as we walk home for dinner. I envy the closeness and the ease of these connections, but every time I feel envy for my daughter, I feel guilty. I decide to take a page from Bell's book and try to start a conversation with the woman standing next to me, who looks like Sofía Vergara.

"How's it going?" I'm nothing if not original.

"Well, you know Delores!" she says, gesturing over her shoulder at any of several women nearby. I don't know Delores. In fact, I had been pretty sure *this* woman was named Delores—I would have sworn it on a stack of humping Bibles, and part of me still suspects it, that she's referring to herself in the third person in that posh way rich people affect.

"Who's that?" I ask, hoping to change the subject. I'm pointing at a bald-headed little girl sitting at the piano, belting out "Let It Go" for all she's worth.

"Last year she hit high C and shattered a crystal champagne flute," possibly-Delores says. Then she leans in conspiratorially. "Betty Armsden heard from Tracy Caplan's oncologist that Marcy's little princess"—she nods at the piano girl, which I'm grateful for because I'm barely following this—"is actually in remission."

I don't understand. "I don't understand," I say. Now is no time to be coy.

"Well, let's just say that some of the girls here shave their heads because they're in chemo, and some of them shave their heads because they want the attention that little girls in chemo get."

I'm actually flabbergasted. I know sometimes when people first go into remission there's a little depression, a little something—the loss of the spotlight, not feeling special anymore, no longer getting all those concerned texts and emails. It can happen to the parents too. But hell, I always just chalked it up to the fact that being in mortal danger lends life a little sparkle that the normal day-to-day just can't maintain. I never thought that anyone would fake it. Or that they would let their kid fake it.

Before I can really process this or ask any of the string of urgent follow-up questions that have occurred to me, possibly-Delores says, "Have you met Maria?" She takes my silence as a negative, which is accurate, and the next thing I know I'm being guided across the room by her tenuous grip on my elbow toward a cluster of completely ordinary but somehow terrifying mothers, one of whom I have to assume will turn out to be Maria.

Maria is trying to connect with me on a diversity level, but she is going about it all wrong.

When I tune back in, what she's saying is this: "Well you know, Hanneke, we were thinking that maybe you would want to play the prince in the final dance." And before I know it there are tears coming out of my eyes. Actual tears. I haven't cried since I heard Tig Notaro was diagnosed with cancer. I rush away from these ladies because I suddenly feel that if I don't get fresh air, I am going to die. I just hope that Bell is somewhere safe and not being molested by one of the dads—is it so wrong to think that? I glimpse what I think is her hair in a nest of young girls tête-à-tête and I'm satisfied, pushing through glass doors and running past the smokers until I am finally and blessedly alone. I pull my phone out of my purse, sending a sheaf of hare-lipped Biafran orphans onto the lawn. A gust takes them away and showers them upon the bouncy castle like a hailstorm even Maleficent herself couldn't have conjured. Me, I'm already dialling my therapist.

"I just cried!" I'm screaming into my phone. "Günter, it's me, and I just cried!" I don't even know yet whether the tears were sad or happy. I mean honestly, that's what our sessions are for. If one of my friends had asked me—hell, if Bell had asked me at home—I would have been all about playing the prince. But something about the way that woman said it ... like it was all I was good for. Like I wasn't a real woman, and couldn't expect to play one.

"Hanneke?" Günter says. "Where are you? What's wrong?"

"I cried!" I scream. Glancing up, I notice a few clusters of mothers looking at me with expressions of concern. I turn the opposite way, toward the flowy vinyl expanse of the bouncy castle, and see more mothers looking at one of my flyers and pointing in my direction. My cover may have been blown.

"Hanneke." Günter's voice is equal parts calming and stern. "I've been trying to reach you since our last session. You need to tell your family about the lump—"

"I have to go, Günter." I hang up, and spin away from all the women glaring at me, and pull open the glass doors to re-enter the fray.

When I walk back in, it's like travelling back in time to my prom. The music is slow and balladic. I can't immediately place it, but I know it's something moving, a romantic scene, slow and saccharine, the kind of dance that movies use to prove that love is real.

"Mommy!" It's Bell's voice, her sweet, lovely little voice, and I hear her before I see her, all the layers of that hideous dress rubbing against each other as she propels herself across the dance floor and into my arms. "Mommy, I didn't know where you were! It's time to dance!"

"I'm right here, baby," I say. She crushes her head into my chest, her hands find mine, and the next thing I know we are swaying in time to this song that I hate. All around me are wigs and bald heads and mothers and fathers and sons and daughters holding each other closely, their mortal worries temporarily suspended. Leaning against the far wall, I see Kyra O'Neil's mother standing alone, checking her makeup in a compact mirror, stoic and beautiful. My daughter's body heat is warming me; the two of us are right here, embracing. And for just the length of one rousing chorus, I feel like everything might be okay.

SIXTEEN SECONDS

SOMETIMES, WHEN I'M feeling stressed out, I take my pulse. It's something my uncle Bill used to do—he was always worried that a heart attack was going to get him, that he'd have some episode of tachycardia that would fail to resolve, and he'd end up clutching his chest and turning blue. But it was lung cancer that got him in the end. Anyway, Bill, he taught me this trick of taking your pulse for ten seconds, then multiplying by six to get the beats per minute. I learned what the normal range was, and it's comforting to know when I'm in it.

These days, I find myself taking it for sixteen seconds and then not bothering with the multiplying. How many heartbeats in sixteen seconds? How many breaths?

There are so many goddamned animal videos on the internet. Yesterday I saw one of a dog playing pool. Not like the paintings on crushed velvet where the dogs sit around tables in neckties playing poker, or are anthropomorphized and holding pool cues. No, this is an actual dog that perches up with its forepaws on the pool table to get the lay of the land, then uses either its paw or its nose to make the shot. And the dog is *good*. The video is edited, of course, so that every shot the dog takes, it sinks. But they are some pretty amazing shots.

David always beat me at pool whenever we played growing up. He always beat me at everything—that's just what older brothers do. He insisted that we call our shots, and he always punched me in the arm if I needed to use the lady's aid. When I was really little I had a habit of turning all the sports words diminutive—I think because I learned *hockey* and *goalie* first, I thought all sports terms ended in an *E* sound. For pool, I would ask if he wanted to be solids or stripies. For basketball, I would ask if he wanted to go shoot hoopies in the driveway. That stuff he never corrected me on.

But he never beat me up so bad as the time I called another kid in my class a fag. He knelt on my head and said, "That's what I am, you doofus." And after that, he called me out any time I was being discriminatory toward queer people, whether consciously or unconsciously.

And I have to say it's genuinely made me a better person. Besides which, chicks dig it when guys are sensitive to stuff like that. I'm pretty sure it's part of why Evie fell for me.

The video is exactly sixteen seconds long, and I often wonder how something so short could have had such an extreme impact on our lives. How something so brief could ripple out and affect all of us for so long.

The video shows my brother in full military gear, holding a dog by the scruff of its neck. He comments on how cute the puppy is. Another Marine steps into the frame and also says the dog is cute. Then my brother winds up, says flatly, "Oops, I tripped," and throws the dog over a cliff into the gulley below. You can hear the dog yelping as it falls, and you can hear the noise the dog makes when it lands. Then the person holding the camera says, "That's just mean, Moreno," and then the video is over.

I emailed David a bunch of times right after it happened. The first couple times I tried to act like everything was normal, like maybe I hadn't seen it. But it was on the goddamned six o'clock news, and all over the internet, and all the papers ran a story about it. If he was getting any of that info over there in the desert, there was no way he didn't know it was all over the rest of the world. So I asked him about it. But I didn't get any answers, and I know from my mom and dad that they didn't either. Which meant that either the emails weren't getting through to him, or he just had nothing to say. And both of those seemed bad.

One of the reasons I love Evie is because she's so relaxed about everything. She hardly ever freaks out or gets stressed out about anything. She's even chill about birth control. Most of the time, when we finish, I'm lying on my back and she's on top of me. When I'm close, she just slides up and off, and my dick flops onto my stomach with that particular slapping sound, and I ejaculate all over myself. It just works for us.

On that first night after the video was posted, I grabbed my T-shirt from the floor to wipe myself off, and Evie snuggled into my side.

"Adam," she said. "Do you think it was real?"

I looked at her, but she had her eyes closed.

"I don't know," I said.

I wanted to say more—like, that if you really look at the dog in the opening frames, it's not moving. It doesn't seem to struggle or twitch. And that when it's flying through the air, the yelping noises sound too close to the camera; they sound fake, or like they were edited in afterward.

But if I said that, I would have to say the rest of it too—that the thud when the dog lands sounds sickeningly final and accurate. And that if the video could be disproven, I was almost sure the Marines would already have gone public with a denial.

"Aren't you going to ask him?"

"I'm not really sure I want to know." I stroked her hair. "And I don't know if he'd tell me the truth."

I expected her to say something else, but nothing came. I wondered what she was thinking, but soon I could tell from her breathing that she was asleep. I didn't fall asleep for a long, long time.

When David was in high school, and when he was getting ready to enlist, he worked out constantly. Lifting weights, running, doing push-ups and sit-ups, all kinds of drills that we would do in the park or after school or just in the basement on the weekends. And I was always there with the stopwatch, tracking his time, handing him his water, and basically helping him out. So it just made sense that I ended up working in a gym, helping people train. I started in high school part-time, then I went through college for kinesiology, and I became a trainer. It's not some big calling, but I don't hate it the way most people I know hate their jobs, and the pay is good enough. Sometimes I worry Evie thinks it's beneath her—like, she's not going to end up with a guy who's just a trainer—but she tells me it doesn't bother her. Some of her more book-smart friends seem to find it pretty funny, but she says she doesn't give a shit what they think, and I guess I have no choice but to believe her.

The thing about my job is that I get to know people without really having to know them. Like, I might see a client for eight weeks at a time, sometimes longer, and so, one or two times a week, I see the same people. We shoot the shit, chit-chat, and I help them work out, tell them what they should eat, and get whatever little tidbits about their lives they want to share with me. But generally I don't hear about their problems, or who they're fucking, or anything too serious.

And with them, it's just first names. I could look up their last names in the computer if I really wanted to, but there's no reason for me to do that. And they just know me as Adam—the only one at the gym. No one has to hear the name Moreno, which has become such a dirty word.

Evie says I need to talk about it. She found me a group to go to, a group for family members of soldiers. She was pretty insistent that

I go. She knows my history with this type of meeting—NA meetings with my mother, Al-Anon to talk about my mother to other addicts' kids—sometimes I'm sick of talking about things in circles. And I don't mean figurative circles, though that's part of it—I mean actual circles of people, with those goddamned folding chairs, always in some basement or rec hall that smells like dust or old feet and burned coffee and desperation. But I'll go, for her.

The group meets on Thursday afternoons, four to six. I don't drink coffee after noon—I try not to drink it at all, it makes my heart race—but they don't have any decaf, or pop, or juice. I ask the volunteer with the name tag if they have any water, and she points me to a sink that's stained with paint and glue, like this used to be a daycare or a place where ex-convicts did arts and crafts to express their feelings. I'm sure the pipes here are lead, and I don't drink tap water in the city as it is. So I take my seat, dry mouthed and with nothing in my hands, so I can't stop myself from fidgeting like everybody else.

There's a nervous energy I don't like, but I'm hoping it will pass once people start talking. There are only two other guys here, one of them so old I'm sure it's his kid he's here to talk about. He has wispy white hair and hearing aids. His face is the kind that just crinkles in different directions—horizontal crinkles across his forehead when he raises his eyebrows in attentive listening, fan-shaped crinkles from his eyes and mouth when he smiles. He doesn't seem to have a natural resting face, it's just permanent movement back and forth between these two expressions, like his face is the leathery folds of a bellows, expanding and contracting with every breath.

The other guy is probably close to my age, maybe even younger, and his hair is dyed black and his nails are painted black and he wears eye makeup. His clothes are black too, and even though there's no metal visible anywhere on him, I'm sure he has piercings in his tongue and nipples and probably other places. Before he even speaks I know he's going to say he cuts himself. He just has that look.

The rest of them are women, women of different ages and shapes and sizes, but they all have open, empathetic faces. I know I'm not going to be able to tell them what David did. These women, they think of their sons and brothers and husbands as puppies to be nurtured and fed and cared for and petted. They don't want to hear my story. They think of soldiers coming back from war as abused dogs that just need a good home and the proper kind of care. They want to blame war for everything—and they should, I blame war too—but they don't want to believe that soldiers can be evil.

The emo kid, I'm surprised to find out, has a mother in the army. And unlike the rest of us, he doesn't have any kind of horror story about her—she isn't injured, and she hasn't committed any major atrocities that he knows about. He just hates the fact she's in the army at all.

"It's embarrassing," he says. "None of my friends' mothers even have jobs, and I always have to explain why mine is away. When I tell them she's in the army people look at me ... they look at me like I'm dirt."

I feel for the kid, because I know he's not going to get much from these people. They tend to be a little more rah, rah, rah.

"You should be proud of your mother's service," one woman says. "It's nothing to be ashamed of."

And then, inevitably, it gets personal: "They probably look at you like that because of all that stuff on your face." This is from the old man. "And that crap on your nails. What are you doing?"

The kid just looks at him. This is when I wish there was a moderator who could handle this sort of conflict in a sensitive way. Instead, this stony silence. I know that I should speak up. David would tell me this is an opportunity to be an ally. This is my chance to protect someone who is being picked on just for being different. Whether this kid likes guys or girls, he has a right to wear nail polish if he wants to, and it wouldn't cost me anything to say so. David would say that this is the very kind of freedom he's over there fighting for.

But I just sit there. Eventually the kid just sniffs and looks at the floor, and one of the moms starts talking about her son.

When a video like this goes on the internet it ends up with its own sort of life—there are spinoffs and responses and analyses. For about eighteen hours, YouTube took the video down, in response to animal cruelty activists who felt it was too graphic. But there were so many copies of it popping up that eventually it became clear taking it down was useless, and then the original video was reposted and easy to find. *Soldier kicks dog off cliff. Soldier throws dog off cliff. Marine throwing dog off cliff in Iraq.* These were the most searched-for terms that whole first week. All you had to do was type *soldier* into the YouTube search bar and it came up as the third suggestion.

I caught Evie watching one of them a few days after the story broke. It was posted by a couple of people who, so far as I can tell, spend their time posting videos of animal cruelty in order to expose perpetrators and raise awareness. They did an almost frame-by-frame analysis of the video to prove that the dog was real. They point to the scruff of its neck that David is holding, how a stuffed dog wouldn't have that. The way the legs move. When David draws back to throw it, the dog's body moves in a realistic way, its hindquarters going back in a way that—and I have to admit this is true—a stuffed dog just couldn't. The people posting the video also contend that the whimpering, though it sounds fake, is actually real, and that experts and veterinarians who work with animals in trauma would tell you that.

I wonder if maybe the dog was already dead when they threw it. Maybe they found a dead dog on the road and decided to make this video. But I don't know if that would be better. And there's nothing visible on the dog—no blood, no bullet hole, no indication of trauma.

At the end of the analysis video, white text comes onto a black screen and calls for the death penalty to be given to the Marines. *These men deserve to die for what they have done. That is my opinion.*

When I read that, a sound came out of me before I could stop it, so Evie turned around and realized I'd been watching her. Her eyes held mine. I wondered what we were going to say to each other. I didn't feel anything except a vague curiosity over what could possibly come next between us.

"Sorry, Adam," she said, then turned the computer off and went and took a shower. When she came out of the bathroom, we didn't talk about it.

I was never so aware of dogs in my life as I was in the days and weeks after the video. One morning after it went up I walked out of the apartment, and within a few feet, I stepped in dog shit. And instead of just being pissed off, I thought, *Dogs are so fucking disgusting.*

And then they were everywhere: tied up outside coffee shops, tied up outside the gym, sitting in cars in parking lots, always panting. They always had their mouths open, tongues lolling out, spumes of drool dropping out of them all the time. They were so frantic, so needy, always begging for something or wanting attention from their owner or whoever was passing by.

We never had a dog growing up; I never learned all the different goddamned breeds of them that people are always going on about, always combining into cuter and cuter names as they interbreed things that have no business humping each other. Maybe that was why David had done it—the dog was rabid, or dangerous, or just annoying. Maybe they didn't have the resources to feed it. Maybe it deserved it.

And honestly, people were dying over there every day—actual human beings, and no one gave a shit about them. Why did people care so much about one goddamned dog?

There was this time that Evie was getting an award for something to do with her graduate degree. It was like, everyone in her program had to write a proposal for a better way to deal with common urban problems, and the top six of them were getting these scholarships that were supposed to help with their degree and also give them some seed money to implement the idea if they wanted. During the afternoon, each of the groups got to present their paper, and it was one of the most boring things I have ever had to sit through. Evie had told me I didn't have to come and she honestly didn't mind—which

I figured was a big old lie—but in the end I wished I'd taken the out because it would have been easier to make that up to her than to sit through all those talks.

After the papers were presented but before the actual awards ceremony, there was a big dinner in a hall. It was buffet style, almost like a wedding, and we all sat at these long tables. One of the students had a visual disability, and she had a helper dog with her, complete with the harness and the vest and all of that. I was down at the other end of the table and probably never would have noticed, except for what happened next.

I guess she'd wrapped the dog's leash around one of the chairs so that he couldn't get very far, and mostly he would just lie down and go to sleep. Well, at some point the lady next to her moved her chair back without being careful and happened to put it down right on the dog's tail. The poor thing yelped and whined—these four high-pitched whines that were *loud.* So loud that everyone in the dining room stopped eating. Evie grabbed my knee. My heart started racing right away, even before we could figure out what had happened.

It was all resolved in a second—the lady moved her chair, and the dog was totally fine, not permanently injured in any way, not even particularly unhappy a couple of moments later. But the quickness with which that silence had descended, the number of people who raised their hands to their throats and mouths, the stricken glances passed around the table, the thudding of my own heart—all from a few loud cries from that dog. We had all reacted to it on instinct.

It could just be a trick of my memory, but I think they sounded exactly like the sounds the dog makes in the video when David throws it off the cliff. How could he do that? Just on an animal level, how? It would be different somehow if the guys seemed to regret it after, if Dave had looked remorseful or upset as the dog spun ass over head through the air. But they all just laugh and shrug, shuffling it off.

I keep wondering how David would have reacted if he'd been at that dinner with me. Maybe there are instincts that some people just don't have?

So many of the stories at group are about the things you'd expect. IEDs. Missions gone awry, resulting in injuries that these men will have for the rest of their lives. One woman goes on and on about her father having multiple sclerosis, how she had to care for him and assist him for most of her life. She'd been so worried her own son would inherit the disease and been ecstatic when he showed no signs of it. Then he enlisted, and he came back missing three of his limbs. And so now she has to do for her son all those same things she did for her father.

Everyone nods with these sympathetic looks and makes little noises in their throats, as if they're smelling something good in the kitchen instead of listening to this woman's pain. She's crying by the end of it, but then she smiles this wide grin and says she feels so much better just talking about it. She was happy to do it for her father, she lies, and she's happy to do it for her son, it's just not how she had envisioned spending her life.

There's a long pause when she's finished, and a few members of the group sort of look at me, encouraging me to take my turn. It's becoming obvious that I'm the only one who hasn't spoken yet, who hasn't told my story. But I don't know how to begin. I know what's happening to me doesn't compare to their stories. I know they won't have any sympathy for me or for my brother.

One of the things I can't stop thinking about is the look on David's face. When I close my eyes I see it. He has this goofy grin, the same grin he used to always get when he was doing something bad. It's that look, more than anything else, that convinces me the video is real. It's the class clown in him, the part of him that loves attention, whether it's good or bad.

And I can't tell whether that makes it better or worse. I recognize him, that's the thing. It's not as if the war has turned into him into this cold-hearted, inhuman weapon that revels in cruelty to animals. He just looks like the same old Dave, doing something stupid to get in with the guys. But how could he be so glib about killing a dog?

After it lands, after that sick thud, the cameraman says to him, "That's just mean." And my brother shrugs. He just shrugs it off with that little grin, as though he's flicked a booger at his teacher or accidentally thrown a baseball through a window.

It terrifies me, because as much as I do recognize him in that look, at the same time I feel like I don't even know him at all. Like maybe I never did.

A couple of weeks after the video went viral, Evie and I went to a dinner party with a bunch of her friends from the university. They all studied things in the humanities, so they were pretty liberal, and they were always having these potlucks. Some of the boyfriends didn't go—the ones who were doctors or lawyers and could blame their work—but there were enough of us guys to make it not seem weird that I was there. Evie always wanted me to go—she said it gave our relationship more weight when we socialized together, and she would make the dish, so there was really nothing for me to do but show up and eat.

The hosts were this couple called Jessica and Norm. Jessica had done a master's in social work and had some kind of job working with disabled people, and Norm was a dentist working for his dad. Their apartment was nicer than ours but not so expensive as to be intimidating. All the food was lined up on a side table where we could serve ourselves, and then we ate from our laps sitting on a combination of couches and the floor. I noticed they didn't even have a TV in their living room.

We talked about all the usual shit, and to be honest it took my mind off the whole business of the video for a while. A couple of people had been travelling in the winter: one couple to an all-inclusive in Mexico, another to do some voluntourism in Haiti. There was a lot of talk about the ethics of travel and what our responsibilities were as First World citizens.

Then, out of the blue, during one of those awkward silences that happen in groups, a girl named Katia with straight black hair and cat-eye glasses cleared her throat and looked at me.

"So, I guess we should talk about the elephant in the room."

I looked at Evie, but she kept her eyes on the floor. There were confused glances going around between the rest of them.

"I just thought we should acknowledge your brother's video," she said. And then she looked at me, and most of the other people turned and looked at me too.

"Uh," I said. "I guess I don't really know what to say."

"What are you talking about?" Norm asked. Jessica put her hand on his knee and gave him a look I couldn't read.

Katia rushed right in. "Adam's brother is a Marine occupying Iraq." Murmurs from around the room.

"It's a peacekeeping mission," I mumbled.

"And he posted a video in which he throws a helpless dog off a cliff. To its death."

Some of the girls gasped, or said "Oh my God" in little whispers. I stared at my socks. My face felt warm, which I knew meant I was turning red. I started to feel my pulse in my temples.

"What do you want him to say?" This was Evie, God bless her. She was behind me on the couch, and I didn't turn to look at her, but I felt her hand on my shoulder. "It has nothing to do with him."

"I guess I was just wondering if you had any insight, or could explain to us why anyone would do something so heinous," Katia said.

Suddenly all the quinoa and black beans and vegan tacos and guacamole threatened to come up. I wanted a beer, but I was driving.

"I don't know. I don't know anything," I said. That Katia girl just kept looking at me, barely blinking. "I haven't heard from him since it went up. They won't ..." I cleared my throat. "They won't let us talk to him. I don't even know if he's getting my emails."

"There's going to be an investigation," Evie said.

Then there was more silence. No one knew what to say from there. I got up and stepped over people so I could go to the bathroom.

"Babe?" Evie asked.

"I'm okay," I said, but I wasn't sure about that at all. I got into the bathroom and started running cold water into the sink. I splashed it on my face, which helped a little with the flush. I put my fingers to my neck and counted, looking at my watch. I got to 18 while the second hand went from 30 to 40. That meant 108 beats per minute. That was high—anything over 90 counted as tachycardia. I took slow, deep breaths. I waited.

Within a couple minutes I could feel my heart rate going down. And suddenly there was music coming from the other room, and I could hear voices, so I could tell they'd moved on. When I opened the door, Evie was there.

"Are you okay?"

I nodded. "I just want to go home."

"Yeah. Okay. I'm sorry."

"Me too."

There's something else that happened that I didn't tell Evie or anyone else. One of David's exes wrote to me and asked to meet up.

I was at work when I got the message, between clients, just screwing around on my phone. I saw I had a message on Facebook from a name that rang a bell, although I couldn't place it. Louis Bundholding. It said: *Hey man, I don't know if you'll remember me, or if David ever mentioned me to you, but I used to hang out with your brother. I'm in the city and just wondered if we could meet up to talk about everything that's going on. I can't believe it and I just want to talk to someone else who knew him.*

I knew he was referring to the video. I had half a dozen other messages from people just trolling me, people who didn't know I was related to David but were just taking a guess based on my name. I wondered how many people named Moreno across the country were getting the same kinds of messages. But this guy knew I was David's brother.

I clicked on his profile, and from the rainbow-flag filters on his friends and a glance at some of his posts, I knew what he meant by "hanging out" with my brother. David had never been one to date a person for long—at least so far as I knew—and he never brought anyone home for dinner or anything like that, even though our mom always told him it would be okay. To me he always made out like he just couldn't commit and was sleeping with dozens of guys all the time, but I always figured he was exaggerating. Or not. I don't really know.

But I had no idea who Louis was. It's not that I was embarrassed to meet up with a gay guy—Evie had gay friends that we were close to, and I really am cool with the whole thing—but I just had no idea what I could say to him. I had no answers, no insights, no secret keys that would unlock the mystery of this whole debacle.

And if I wanted to talk, I had group for that.

In group, nobody knows my last name. We don't even know if each other's first names are real, though I told them I was Adam that first week because I couldn't think of anything else. No one has mentioned the video or the incident, which is almost conspicuous, because in every other area of my life except the gym, it seems to be all anyone is talking about. But even if they've seen it, without a last name they have nothing to tie me to it. David is wearing a helmet and desert goggles, and you don't see much of his face, and we don't look similar enough that anyone could ID me just from that.

"That's just mean, Moreno." That's what the cameraman says at the end of the video, and that's how my brother was identified as the perpetrator, and that's how everyone knows I'm his brother. Lance Corporal David Moreno, and me his baby brother Adam. Most of the time, I'm mad at that guy, whoever he is—why did he have to say our last name? Even if he'd just said "Dave," no one would have connected me to it.

It's my third week at the group and I'm the only one who hasn't spoken. Shared. The old guy, Alan, has talked about having all three of his sons in service and abroad, the moms have all cried and held each other and told their terrible stories, and the emo kid has complained about his soldier mom two different times. I have a feeling they aren't going to let me get away with sitting through another meeting without saying something myself, and it turns out I'm right.

"Adam." The woman who says it is named Maria or Marina or Marita, I can never seem to hear it clearly, no matter how many times she repeats it. "We haven't heard from you yet. Please, tell us your story."

Everybody looks at me with those faces, waiting to hear my sad story. They must mean well, but how will they stop themselves from comparing my story to theirs, to quantifying their pain against mine?

"My brother's in Iraq," I say, and already there are nods and encouraging gestures. A fat blond lady who always clutches Kleenexes is already dabbing at her eyes.

I start talking then, and a river of bullshit comes out of me. I don't tell them about the video, the dog, or David. I tell them that my brother was a sniper, and that he had to kill women and kids who were carrying explosives, and that when he got home the PTSD was so bad that he shot himself in our garage. I swear I didn't plan it. It just comes out so fast, just a few quick sentences. And before I know it I'm crying, and the fat woman is hugging me, and Marina is looking pleased with herself. An older woman named Sylvia tells about when her sister committed suicide, and then the meeting moves on, and then it's over.

That night, Evie gets home late. I'm already in bed, waiting for her. The apartment's mostly dark except for one lamp that bathes her corner of the room in a yellow triangle of light, so she can see to lock the door and make her way over to the bedroom, to the bathroom. She's moving quietly, because she thinks I might be asleep. I hear her brushing her teeth, peeing without flushing the toilet, so the noise won't wake me. I love her.

She pulls back the covers, and a sluice of cold air touches my body. Then she is in bed beside me with the covers thrown over her, and my heat starts to warm us both as she snuggles up to my side. I touch her hair, her cheek, and we kiss.

I can taste the minty residue of toothpaste, but beneath it there's white wine and something savoury. She makes a little noise as I swirl my tongue around her mouth, and she swings a leg over me and climbs on top. I'm hard already and she takes me inside her without even taking off her T-shirt, and I haven't even opened my eyes, but I feel so happy and so safe.

It's quick and warm, and I slide my hands down to her hips, but she's doing most of the work. It's only a couple minutes, but we both know sometimes that's all it takes; we just want to get off before falling asleep.

I feel her tense as she goes to lift herself off of me, but I keep my hold on her hips and resist.

"I thought you were close," she says, still moving up and down.

"I am." I throw my head back as I say it, my pillow puffing out around my head and almost covering my ears.

"Adam," she says. I can't tell if the tone in her voice is a warning or an encouragement to keep going. She rises up again with a little whimper, but I hold her down, close to me—I'm strong and it's easy to hold her there—and I thrust, and we both finish. It's intense.

"Jesus, what were you thinking?" She says this as she's snuggling up to my side, nestling in for the night. "We have to be careful." She slaps me lightly on my shoulder, a playful reprimand for risking our future on a few extra seconds of bliss.

"I know we do," I mumble. "Sorry." She makes a sleepy little sound like it's all right.

I turn toward her, and put my arm around her, and hold her close.

SOMETHING ADJACENT TO THE F-SLUR

I WILL ADMIT that this was my first time attending a meeting of the board of the hockey league, and I was only there out of duty and obligation as mother of the accused. Apparently my son was in some kind of trouble for the language he was using. To be honest, I tuned out a fair amount of what went on before they got to the actual topic that concerned us, me and my son. I was still having trouble believing what they were saying about him.

"I don't think we should just be addressing Daniel's isolated comments," some woman is saying now. "There's actually been a fair bit of homophobia noticed throughout the league."

"That's a very general statement. Would you care to be more specific?" This is from Donald Fogarty, who is so old and has been on the board for so long that I swear I would believe he was having a similar meeting about whether to allow Black kids into the league fifty years ago. And I'm not at all sure which side of that issue he would have fallen on.

"We have very strict policies about language and tolerance in our league," he begins. "We banned the F-slur years ago."

"What the hell is the F-slur?" This is from a ball cap–wearing dad near the back.

"When the kids don't do well in their drills, their coach calls them faggots."

The word kind of hovers in the air for a moment, everyone silent and blinking. Don rubs his hand over his eyes and lets out a sigh that sounds tired and old.

"That's not true," Don starts to say. "Coaches are not permitted—"

"Don't try to say it isn't true!" Another woman jumps in. "We've all heard it. My daughter came home and asked me what that word meant. I had to explain it to her. Can you imagine that? An eight-year-old girl, with a gay uncle she's always loved, and I'm sitting there trying to explain to her what a faggot is."

"Please refrain from saying the F-slur at this meeting," the second-in-command says. Don nods his assent. "We must conduct this meeting according to the same rules we ask our players and coaches to abide by."

"I thought they were supposed to say 'maggots' now instead? Because it's more inclusive?" This from a balding dad I'm willing to bet my Michael Kors wristwatch on has been divorced for much longer than he was ever married.

"How is 'maggots' more inclusive?" This is from the ball-cap dad again.

"We're all adults here, and if we're talking about kids saying the word *faggot,* we should be able to say it too!" I couldn't see who said this, and just from the voice it was hard to tell if it was a man or a woman.

"For clarity," Don said, "the term used by Daniel was not the F-slur itself, but something adjacent to the F-slur that was first used against the son of two proud dads and then on another occasion against a player who was conceived through sperm donation. The word used was *fagspawn.*"

Several people gasp, and I must admit that I feel my stomach lurch. It's just so graphic, and so awful. And I don't have a clue where Daniel could have heard it—certainly not from me. I wonder how he's doing. They've relegated him to another room with some of the younger kids whose ears were deemed too tender for the meeting. He's probably on his phone, even though he knows we're in here deciding his fate.

"This league is supposed to be fun," someone else has started saying. "I can't believe we even have to talk about this." Then things descend into chaos for a bit, before order at the meeting is restored.

If there's anything I'll say about Daniel's father, Stanley, it's that once he became his true self, he never looked back. That's the thing I still admire about him, the reason I can still love him despite everything that's happened. He even makes the name Stanley *sound* gay, with a bit of a sibilant *S* at the beginning, using the "-ley" to add flair, as though those three letters are a fan he's wafting over his entire being in a showy, demonstrative manner.

He'd be the first to point out that showy and demonstrative mean the same thing.

Surprisingly, for someone as gay as he is, Stanley is nearly allergic to frills. He hates redundancy, because he thinks life is too short. I think only people who feel they have wasted whole decades of their lives on something feel that way. For me, life feels monotonous and never-ending, like I'm stuck in one of those time loop movies that come out every couple of years. My days are startlingly similar. Even the years take on a certain homogenous wash, where I can't tell one from the other. Next year might as well be last year might as well be now … the only thing that changes are my haircuts, and even then, it's minimal.

People get defensive on my behalf when I use language like that, saying that Stanley wasted a decade of his life with me. It's hard to explain to them that I don't feel offended by it, that it's my word, because in lots of ways I feel like that time with Stanley was a waste, for me too. We just got together too young, we didn't know what it was supposed to feel like, so even though it was so obviously wrong, we just kept going. I think a lot of people do that. I think a lot of people are together who shouldn't be, because they're just too afraid to try anything else, or to be alone. And I guess if I'm being honest, I fall into that category too.

And depending which way the conversation is going, we always get into who gave Daniel to whom. "But he gave you your son," people say, when they want to defend Stanley. "But you gave him his son," people say, when they want to show they support me and that I am clearly in the right. The truth is, we give our children to each other. It's a weird little conspiracy that parents have, deciding to create another life, without any way of asking that person if they want to exist at all.

Daniel, of course, is very good at expressing the fact that he doesn't want to exist. That he didn't ask to be here. Hockey is one of the only social activities he likes, and his only form of exercise of which I am aware, so I am very much invested in his being able to continue to play in the league.

When I was brought up, we would have considered Daniel's position on his life to be suicidal ideation. We would have said he needed counselling. But these days, the feedback I'm getting is that his feelings are normal.

"Lots of young people today don't want to be alive," Melissa tells me. "They don't really feel there's a future. You know, because of the climate nonsense."

A few weeks ago, Paula emailed to tell me the most recent news about her son: He was tied to a tree for five minutes when the recess monitors weren't looking, and the kids who tied him up took turns punching him.

The tying detail really gets to me—I'm claustrophobic and don't like being restrained, I can't even wear turtlenecks comfortably—and the idea of being restrained while being hit just wrecks me. It's one thing when someone is holding you down, the way an overly aggressive lover might, because you can feel them struggle, feel the ebb and flow of their strength pitted against yours.

But being tied up, that just felt so inhumane to me—I've never let anyone tie me up, and I never would. To be honest, what her story brought to mind for me was Matthew Shepard, the gorgeous young man who was tied to a fence and beaten and left for dead in Laramie, Wyoming. It happened when I was in university, and there was a made-for-TV movie about it that I remember watching with my friends. I forgot all about it for years, but once Stanley started introducing me to his new friends, I found out all the gay men of our generation are obsessed with this story, because the guys who did it had lured Matthew by pretending they were interested in him romantically.

But I don't tell any of this to Paula when I write her back—why would I? To what possible end? I know she worries already that her son might be queer, or at least gender nonconforming, like everyone his age, and I know she worries about his dating prospects as an adult, given where he sits on the spectrum. It seems to me that all we do as parents is worry, that having children just means you stop worrying about yourself and only worry about your kids for the rest of your life.

❖ ❖ ❖

The second-in-command has invited concerned parents to speak at the microphone about why they think my son should or shouldn't be allowed to say in the league. They have said, "The young man's mother is in attendance," but they didn't specifically point me out, and I wonder how many people know.

The man at the microphone now introduced himself as Billy, which I find a silly name for a grown man. He is attacking my son's character:

"If the mouse wasn't in the wall, it couldn't come out the hole."

"What?" Don Fogarty has lost all semblance of patience.

"It's Latin."

"That sure as Christ wasn't Latin, Billy."

"Well, I'm translating. It's a Latin idiom. Like when people use the excuse that they were drunk when they said something racist or misogynist. But the idea is, well, if the mouse wasn't in the wall, it couldn't come out the hole."

A murmur of assent bubbles through the crowd. I think he's talking utter nonsense. There's no Latin expression like that I've ever heard of, and I was a classics major. As he walks by me I whisper, "*Tamquam mus in matella,*" which means "like a mouse in a chamber pot," which is an actual literary reference to something written in Latin. It means someone stuck in an unpleasant situation. Which is definitely how I'm feeling. For the first time, I wish Bernie were here with me.

"My dad wasn't good at anything," Bernie told me once. "Except maybe drinking." We were watching Daniel's hockey game, and he'd just been pulled off the ice after being on the receiving end of a questionable check.

I thought Bernie was being a little dramatic, as well as taking focus away from the issue at hand, which was Daniel, though of course I wasn't there when Bernie was growing up, and this was an unsupportive thing for me to be thinking.

I wondered what my dad would have thought, seeing my son like this, so pissed off about being pulled and gearing up for another fight. I knew that if he was injured, he would lie about it just to get back on the ice. That's how badly he wanted it. I could never care that much; to me it was always just a piece of vulcanized rubber sliding across the ice. I could never really get into the team sports thing, the way people supposedly see the nobility of all things human in team sports, as if agreeing on these rules, even for a short period of time, somehow melts away our differences and makes us one. I always thought that was preposterous.

"You're letting your trauma speak for you," was something my therapist loved to say. She also encouraged me not to think of her as a therapist so much as a "spiritual counsellor," someone who could advise me, nudge me in the right direction, and help me slowly on my way. Her name was Minerva, though I suspect she made that up.

"When you react with the same pain as you've always felt," Minerva told me, "you feed that pain and help to keep it alive. Instead, acknowledge the pain and try to move through it."

Bernie came into my life all at once. I wish I could say that I hadn't kept a hole there, a space, a concavity that was just waiting for him to fill. It wasn't just the space that Stanley left, it was bigger; I'd made it bigger by the time Bernie came along. It was like I grew into a shape that always left my life with space, like when a tree bifurcates around something, except that rock or whatever it is, in my life it's just a space. I don't know how to be a whole person, that's how it feels. When I'm alone I'm just bored, and everything feels pointless. It can feel like that with Bernie too, or with Daniel if I'm being honest, but then at least there's someone else to blame. And someone else to suffer with. Anything is better than suffering alone.

People go on so much about awareness these days, as though being aware of something can help you to change it. I get how it's the first step, but it's not the most important one, and really it should barely count toward actually changing the behaviour. I'm aware of the things I'm not doing in my life, and aware of the things I'm doing wrong, and aware of everything I want to change. I just don't know how to do it, and most days I don't even think I have the ability. Self-improvement is such a bitter lie.

I don't even need to be thriving, or doing so much better than I already am; I just want to be less actively self-destructive.

The reason I'm saying that is because I can see what I was doing with Bernie. He's every inch a man. He's a manly man, even. I hate that I still think in those terms, but I can't deny that I do. I want to say that he eats red meat, but he hasn't since his cholesterol started going up. He's not brutish ... or, at least, he's brutish in ways that turn me on. It takes a certain kind of woman to accept the kind of man that she likes. He's not what I'm supposed to like, not what my girlfriends think is best for me.

"At least he takes care of you," Roxanne says. She means sexually rather than financially. She's my sister, and the only person I talk to about sex, although even then it makes me very uncomfortable. I have to have a good amount of rosé before I can bring it up. She's much more comfortable with it, because she went through a slut phase and sometimes regresses back into it. We can talk about how we dealt with the trauma we inherited from our father in different ways, and how the trauma he directly inflicted on us is similar or different given our birth order and our individual personalities and roles within the family.

Stanley was the opposite of brutish. He got regular paycheques that were always the same predictable amount, and he took care of all the books. Everything we had was nice, and worked properly, and was paid for. I never lacked for anything, but everything felt wrong all the time. No one tells you that life can feel like that, or what to do when it does. And then they try to tell you that it's you, that you have depression, that you need a hobby, that you have unrealistic expectations of marriage … until it turns out that your husband is gay.

I couldn't imagine Stanley being gay, because I couldn't imagine him being anything so interesting. We didn't have gay friends, or gay relatives, or even nieces or nephews that we speculated about. We were boring, normal people. Sometimes I think that was the root of the betrayal. It's not that his desire for me had been a lie, it's that he was capable of desiring these other things, something so different, that he even had the capacity for such an original and unprecedented craving. How had he figured out the shape and object of his desire?

I wanted to try women as revenge. Or, more accurately, I wanted to want to try women as revenge. My mind thought this would be great, and would test how accepting and alternative Stanley had really become. Him having a boyfriend was one thing, but how would he respond when I swanned in with a woman in a leather jacket and talked about the way her motorcycle vibrated between my legs? But my body wouldn't cooperate; I just couldn't get aroused, thinking about women. Even the ones who looked hot in photos weren't people I could imagine myself sleeping with. So I was once again the boring one, and the one who would be left behind as Stanley pranced into a life of literal rainbows and glitter. While it didn't seem a natural environment for the Stanley I knew, it still felt like he was getting the better end of the deal. He got a new identity and new friends and supposedly a sense of fulfillment that I could probably never understand. And I got to start over.

To say that Bernard and Daniel were friends or even friendly would be an overstatement, I know. But saying they were enemies would be totally inaccurate. Again, I don't feel like I know what is supposed to be normal in these situations. No one gets along with their stepparents. Women love their stepchildren, don't they? Or they can convincingly pretend to. Men who are stepfathers just need to know when to be absent and when to lend the odd paternalistic word without being threatening. And I trusted Bernie with that, I really did. He had raised his own kids, and they were boys, and every one of them was straight.

People are surprised when their partner turns out to be racist, or to hate any sort of minority group. But how would you know? That is, unless you expose them to every kind of minority while you're dating, unless you bring up specific things and ask them about it, how do you ever find out? As I said, no one in my life was gay, beyond some college acquaintances I didn't talk to anymore. The fact that Stanley was now gay was an obvious exception, an aberration that was never anticipated or courted. If Bernie was standoffish with Stanley, I chalked it up to normal jealousy. Stanley is my first love and my ex-husband; of course I didn't expect my new husband to cozy up to him. And even if it was *because* Stanely was gay, he didn't say or do anything overtly homophobic. It's not like he ever made comments that I could interpret that way.

I'm sounding defensive again, and I know it. And if I sound that way to myself, what am I going to do when it's actually time to open my mouth?

❖ ❖ ❖

In the end, I don't have to address the crowd with some kind of speech. They have an impromptu vote about letting Daniel stay, during which I, of course, raise my hand with the ayes. They say that as long as there is a talk between the parents and the player in question, and he promises not to use offensive language in the future, he should be given a chance to stay.

After the meeting, I, the parent present, have that talk with my taciturn teenage son, and Don Fogarty, and two other people from the board. They seem fixated on getting to the bottom of where the slur came from.

"Where did you hear that word, Daniel?"

It's hard to describe what's in his eyes, but they're driving into me like drill bits, with something like anger, something like hate, something I want to find a portion of regret in, but when I think that, I'm kidding myself. He knows that I've put him in a corner where he has to say words that hurt me, and he will never forgive me for it.

"It's what Bernie calls me when you're not around."

His eyes are back on his shoes, and he's not the only one. The silence is heavy in the room, and I feel like I'm stuck in aspic.

Don Fogarty is the one who breaks it. "And who is Bernie?"

"Bernie is my husband," I say. No one reacts. I still feel like I'm suffocating.

"Who is Bernie … to Daniel?"

"He's my stepdad," Daniel says. And someone gasps. Later I will spend so much time trying to figure out which one of them it was, but I can't tell in the moment. There are just eight eyes staring at me, waiting for me to say something that will make it all make sense.

THE MINE MONSTER OF BRITANNIA BEACH

I. 1942

IT WASN'T FAIR that Vanessa didn't get to go work in the mine too; she was just as strong as her brothers, Father had even said so.

But the mine was just for the men. And she was a girl, and only twelve years old, at that. Yet, no matter what else she got up to in the course of her day, the mine was never far from her thoughts.

Mother had caught her a few years ago, after she took the sewing scissors and trimmed down a paper plate to the size of a saucer and glued it to one of her headbands, worn horizontally across her forehead to look like a miner's light. She had also smeared black smudges of her mother's mascara across her cheeks and forehead.

"What are you doing?" Her mother's voice had sharpness to it, but Vanessa, deep in her game, missed the warning.

"I'm playing miner," she answered.

Her mother grabbed the headband off of her so fast that the ends of it left scratches along Vanessa's temples. She ripped off the paper plate and crumpled it in her hand.

"The mine is not a joke!" Her mother raised her hand as if to smack her, and Vanessa squealed and shrank back, eyes widening even as small beads of blood formed along the scratches on her face. Instead her mother clenched her hands even tighter and brought her nose within an inch of Vanessa's own. "How dare you go through my things and take my makeup? That's not free, you know! And now you've wasted it on your ugly face." She grabbed the thin tube of mascara and started out of the room. She paused in the doorway, but didn't look back. "I don't know how you could do that," she said quietly. "I don't know how you could do that when you know what happened to Mark."

Vanessa wiped her face with water from a bowl and an old face-cloth, but it was hard to get the black stuff off. She probably needed soap, but she didn't want to go all the way to the kitchen or the bathroom to get it. She rubbed her face until it was red and splotchy, all the while trying to see in the mirror if she was ugly, which her mother had never said to her before. Father said she was *cute as a button*, but she didn't know how cute that was, and she didn't trust Father to know about something like beauty more than her mother. When Randal got home, she was going to ask him, because he knew everything about everything.

Randal was her oldest brother, twenty-three years old, and he was her most favourite person in the whole family and the whole town. On the days when they got paid, Father would buy six beer. Of these he kept two for himself, gave one to Mother, and gave one each to Randal and James and Francis. James would drink his right away, often in one long gulping swallow, which mother called *uncouth*. Francis poured his into a glass and sipped it during dinner, and sometimes he would hold his little finger out until Father told him not to. Randal would wait until well after dinner was over. He would crawl out of his bedroom window to sit on the roof, looking out at the lights twinkling on the side of the mountain like stars in the black night, and he would let Vanessa snuggle up to him sometimes. His eyes would get bright and wet, and his mouth would twist into a sideways smile, and his words would get funny and a little jumbled. If she asked him about the mine then, in just the right quiet way, without looking straight at him, he would tell her stories of the other men, the dripping, black cavern, what it felt like to be so deep inside the earth. But mostly he talked about leaving Britannia Beach, about where he wanted to go in the world.

When Vanessa crept out onto the roof that night, it was cold enough that she could see her breath right away. She cozied up to Randal and he put his arm around her, and she felt warm everywhere except her fingers and the tip of her nose.

"Mom called me ugly today."

Randal just took a long swig of his beer and kept staring out into the night.

"She said I have an ugly face." Still he wasn't saying anything. So maybe it was true.

“Your face isn’t ugly,” Randal said, after what felt like forever. “But playing that game is. She told us all about it. You know why she was upset, don’t you?”

“Because of Mark.” Everything bad was because of Mark. It wasn’t Vanessa’s fault that the monster at the bottom of the mine had eaten him up.

“That’s right. That’s why you shouldn’t talk about the mine to Mama.”

“But you and Dad and James and Francis go there every single day,” she pleaded.

“We do it because we have to,” he said. That was it for a while, other than the wind and the odd coyote and the sound of the ocean from way down at the shore. After he had his last swallow—she could always tell it was the last one, because he held the bottle up to his face for longer, trying to get out every drop—he put his hand on her head and said, “Besides, little sister, we mine copper, not coal. There’s no black dust down there, so there’s no need to go rubbing that stuff all over your face.”

This seemed like enough new information for one night, and later, as Vanessa lay in her own bed waiting for sleep, she thought about copper and how it shone and wondered why her brothers didn’t come out of the earth glittering like diamonds.

Over the next three years, Vanessa and Randal came to share lots of secrets. She trusted him because he was the only one who would talk to her about all the things that were really going on, all the things the mine monster did that everybody else was too afraid to talk about. He hadn’t been alive when the avalanche destroyed the

Jane Camp, because that was back in 1915, but he knew all about all the families that got killed. He was four when the mill burned down, and he said he could still remember the orange flames against the black sky. Vanessa believed him because she was four on the day when Mark didn't come home, and she still remembered little bits about his face and his laugh, and how Mama looked when she turned pale and quiet and cried. And later that year that Randal was four, a big flood washed half the houses away, and thirty-seven people died. And everyone blamed the monster. No one ever talked about it much, except for Randal.

Randal trusted Vanessa because he had to, because she was the only one in the family other than Mother who didn't work in the mine. Mother and Father didn't know it, but Randal wanted to be a doctor. And he was taking part of the money he earned and sending away for courses from universities, and learning all the things he needed to know before he would go away forever to study medicine. Randal would ask Vanessa to make sure she got to the mail before Mother did, so she could pluck out any letters addressed to him and put them in his dresser drawer for him to read at night when he got home.

That summer that she was twelve, he asked her to pick up a parcel for him, a microscope he had ordered that he needed for his courses, which were starting to get more advanced. Mama was used to Vanessa picking up the mail at this point, and so she set off for town feeling like she was doing something important, trying to figure out how she was going to get the microscope into the house unseen.

It had only been a year or two since her mother let her walk places on her own. The post office was a little building not far from the general store, where you could send a telegram (if you had the money to do it and someone to send it to and something important to say, that's what Mama always said), and where Mr. Barrow would give her bundles of letters tied with twine, letters from Mother's sisters all around BC and two in Ontario, and sometimes from Mother's brother's wives in Calgary and Edmonton, and from Father's mother down in the South of the USA, and the letters for Randal. But today, when Vanessa was expecting a parcel, something that could be a microscope (she only had the most basic understanding of what one was, from things she'd read and an illustration Randal had shown her in a catalogue and what he'd told her about how it would let him see things that were very, very small—in fact, he'd promised that if she got it home in one piece, he would let her look at her blood with it, an idea that thrilled her and scared her in a way she couldn't quite name), all she got was a piece of paper. She struggled to make out the words—she *could* read, better than Father even, but the type was faint and there were long strings of letters and numbers she couldn't understand. She showed Mr. Barrow and asked him what it meant.

"For a parcel this size, you have to go to the train station, dear." He pointed to the numbers. "This here is a special tracking number—make sure that matches with the parcel you receive. Do you know the way?"

Of course she did. She knew where everything was in the whole town. Ever since Mother had let her out on her own, she'd been exploring. She knew how to get to the new bowling alley, and the billiards hall, the swimming pool and the tennis courts, and she knew that those were the main things people did for fun. She knew how each road and pathway connected with the others, and she even knew shortcuts through the forest that could be taken on foot, while the heavy vehicles had to stay on the switchbacks, where things were steep.

She calculated that she still had time to get to the railway station and back home in time to help Mother with dinner. She headed down, and she had to go past the Parsonses'. Bart Parsons had been the last one the monster at the bottom of the mine had gotten. Vanessa remembered Mrs. Parsons all dressed in black, her face puffy and red from crying. Walking by the house was giving her a funny, creepy feeling. She kept turning behind her to see if she was being followed, but there was nobody there. It got to the point where she was turning around every few steps, and she felt silly. She wanted to break into a run, but Mother had told her only little girls run in public, and young ladies must walk with poise and grace. But she guessed the monster didn't care. It suddenly seemed important to her to know whether the monster was *only* in the mine, or if it could leave and go other places in the town. If it could get out, that would explain a lot of things. Maybe it was the monster who had killed the Fenwicks' horse, which a year ago had been found dead and drained of blood. Maybe the monster had eaten the baby the McKinnans said had died in its sleep. But if the monster could crawl out of the mine and go wherever it wanted, then she wasn't totally safe on these walks around the town. She had to keep her guard up.

Finally she could see the train station below her, and it was all she could do not to run the last ten feet there. But she kept her cool, and walked over to the counter and handed her slip to the man—she'd seen him at church but didn't know his name.

"Please, sir, I'm here to pick up this package. It's for my brother."

The man smiled kindly. "You wait here while I go and fetch it," he said. "And don't mind him. He's headed off to protective custody with the rest of them."

She wondered what he meant until a dragging metal sound startled her. She turned, and saw what at first she'd taken for a bundle of rags. Then it shifted, and she realized it was a crouched man with a chain around his ankle. The chain was attached to a heavy wrought-iron bench, dragging on the floor with a padlock on it. She was startled, and she made a sound.

The man looked at her then. He had squinty eyes but she could tell he was staring right at her. For a second, she wondered if he was sad. Then he bared his teeth at her and hissed. She screamed. He laughed and laughed and rattled his chains. She was safe. He couldn't get her.

The man came back, holding a box wrapped in brown paper.

"Here you go," he said. He handed it to her, and she was surprised by how heavy it was. She couldn't stop looking at the man who was chained up and squatting. She didn't know if it would be impolite to ask about him.

So she thanked the man behind the counter and began to walk home, careful to carry the package with both hands and look where she was going as she went back up the side of the mountain.

II. 1981

The thing Vanessa hated most about her therapist's office—well, she couldn't begin that thought, couldn't quantify—enumerate?—couldn't rank all the things she hated about therapy; all of them were equally superlative. It made her so aware of herself (the irony was not lost on her); suddenly her body language *meant* something, things she forgot *meant* something, the very words she chose when she spoke *meant* something. Everything had meaning there, and everywhere else her life had none.

The therapy was a court-appointed condition, one of the only reasons she had been spared going to jail—thank God for that, can you imagine? She didn't know what would have happened to her there. But sometimes she wondered if it might have gone the other way. At least it would have been something different. How would she have fared in there, in prison, with all those hard ladies from unfortunate backgrounds who were so tough and so different? She knew it was a fantasy, but she liked to think she would have done just fine. Surprised them all. But even if she'd crumbled, even if she'd had to cry herself to sleep every night and endure terrible cruelties at the hands of the other inmates, at least it would have been interesting. At least it would have been new. And at least it would have been something different, an actual real consequence for hitting that poor boy with her car.

"You mustn't blame yourself, Vanessa," the therapist was saying. "You must stop with all this blame." Vanessa thought it was a silly prospect and didn't see how they were going to make any progress at all if the therapist continued to insist on pursuing this line of reasoning. "Who else could possibly be to blame?" Vanessa had asked on her first visit. "I was the one driving the car. I quite literally did it." The therapist kept insisting that it was an accident, which was plain enough, but the fact that no one had planned it didn't make Vanessa any less culpable. A different person driving—or no one driving at all—and that child would still be alive. She didn't see the point in trying to make nice about it, or to pretend otherwise. She'd done what she'd done and was willing to pay for it. The punishment, it seemed, was coming twice a week to see this woman who kept insisting that it wasn't Vanessa's fault after all.

Vanessa had been moving things in the office when her therapist wasn't looking. She'd be writing notes in her yellow legal pad, just like the lawyers had at the seemingly endless series of depositions and statement-giving sessions and declarations of fact that happened after the accident, and while she was taking notes in her messy handwriting—*scrawling*, really, that stereotype seemed to apply to all types of doctors—Vanessa would turn a bust to face the other way, or flip a book so the pages showed out instead of the spine, or simply drag her finger through the dust on the bookshelves.

That was how it had started, actually, first just leaving lines in the dust, then writing *DUST ME* and thinking later with glee about the embarrassment it would cause. Then she started drawing obscene things in the dust, a giant penis attached to hairy testicles, just as someone had left in the grime on her car once, when she'd had to go to a *plaza* in a rush, instead of her usual shops. But the doctor never mentioned it. She never said anything at all. And so Vanessa supposed she had a maid. She supposed when you made as much money as the psychiatrist presumably did that you didn't clean your own office but hired a service or, at the very least, some immigrant lady to do it for you. (She wondered if the doctor cleaned her own house or if she hired that out too. Did she even cook for her husband, or did she pay someone to do all the things she couldn't because of her job?) It wasn't always dusty in the office, of course, so on those weeks she'd figure out something else to do.

And yet the doctor never noticed it. Sometimes the objects were still facing the wrong way the next time she showed up, sometimes they'd been moved back. Probably the cleaning woman did it, or else the doctor, if she noticed at all, presumed that the cleaning lady had moved things the wrong way around. She wasn't so clever then, this therapist; she didn't see or notice as much as she fancied she did, even with all her expensive degrees on the wall behind her. What did she really know about the world at large, or about Vanessa, if she couldn't even keep track of things within her own office? She only knew what Vanessa chose to tell her, which wasn't the whole story at all.

III. 2015

Vanessa sat in her apartment, trying to think of the last time she'd had a visitor in it, someone other than her own children, who came rarely. And they—her children—were already in their fifties, the oldest of their own children starting high school in the fall, all of them hours away by car. This young man, in his twenties—which these days, from what she could gather, was a decade spent in an ineffectual parody of adulthood—seemed totally out of place in her grim, tired apartment. She wondered if she should turn on more lights, something she never did when she was alone.

Why had he come? She couldn't imagine what would have possessed him to do that, to look her up after all these years, out of nowhere, when they'd barely even met as adults. Randal had been dead for eight years, and she'd never expected to see any of his children again, let alone his grandchildren. But here she was, opening her door, making tea for this young man who had sent her an email and suggested a visit.

She looked for her brother in him, wasn't sure whether she saw him there or not. She'd barely known Randal, after all. Her memories of him were those of a child, and so she knew they couldn't be trusted.

"He left when I was only fifteen," she told the young man. "I didn't see him again for another thirty years."

"He used to tell a story that you didn't wave goodbye when he left," he said. For a second she couldn't remember his name—all she could think of was Randal. But Randal had looked older at this age. This boy was unmarried, and his skin was so smooth that it was clear he'd barely lived at all.

"It's a lie, Michael," she said. His name had come back to her. "I cried when he left." She remembered this clearly. She had been proud of him, even understanding as little as she did, and she'd known it would be a long time before she saw him again, and he was her favourite brother.

It was silent for a bit then, both of them sipping their tea, wondering what they could possibly find to say to one another.

It had been so long since she'd had someone around who was related to her—related but a stranger—someone who was obliged to politely care about her, but with whom she didn't have any history or, more poignantly, any responsibilities. She didn't have to be a mother or a grandmother or cosset him in any way, unless she felt like it. Because he was young and a man he needed some nurturing, of course: He was hungry—or at the very least he could eat, men could always eat—and so far he had cleared a plate of sliced cheese and Ritz crackers, and another of shortbread cookies, and had three cups of tea—it was more than she ate in two days sometimes—and she could see shiny patches on the knees of his pants, and his shirt was in want of ironing. It had been so long since she'd done those things for a man, Roger having been dead twenty-five years already.

She was enjoying talking, the sound of her own voice, which sometimes she didn't use for weeks at a time. She'd never formed a habit of talking to herself out loud—Roger had considered it self-indulgent, and she'd agreed wholeheartedly. There was an album she'd been working on, with old pictures she'd found, writing down what she could remember, and it kept swimming up into her mind as she was chit-chatting about the family and making him nod politely. But something was stopping her from showing it to him. She didn't know if she could trust him, this grandnephew of hers—was that the term? What a ridiculous thing. Young people had no sense of privacy or what was appropriate anymore.

When she had nothing else in her cupboards to feed him but sensed that he was somehow still hungry, in need of something substantial, they walked over to a small park just a few hundred feet away. In this park was a small café that sold hot dogs and hamburgers, and she watched him eat a cheeseburger and french fries with a fantastic amount of ketchup. When he ate, it wasn't Randal he reminded her of so much as Francis; there was something dainty about the way he did it, dabbing at the corners of his mouth with the paper napkin between bites.

Back in her apartment, she wondered again about showing him the album, but decided against it. But her mind kept swirling back to those early years of her life in Britannia Beach, and he seemed interested in them.

"I don't know if you're aware, but the government has been cleaning it up there," he told her. "They've sighted orcas and dolphins in Howe Sound again."

"What do you mean, cleaned up?"

"From the pollution, from the mine. There were heavy metals in the water."

"The stream there was always crystal clear," she told him. She remembered that very well.

"That's because nothing could live in it," he said. He said it in that way young people have when they think they're being gentle and avoiding insult, when really there's nothing worse. Maybe the mine had been polluting the water, she didn't know. She noticed, though, how the possibility made her feel angry. But she was past the age where she needed to express it, especially to this young man who probably didn't care how she felt, anyway.

"Do you want to go see it?"

She was sure she hadn't heard him correctly. Go to Britannia Beach? The idea had never occurred to her, even though it was less than an hour away by car. He had a rental car, that was what he was saying, one of those new hybrid kinds, and he was willing to take her.

"There's a mining museum there now," he said—which was true, she had heard that, or read about it in the paper. "Maybe we could find a picture of my grandfather. Or of your father."

She was going to say that she had plenty of pictures of both his grandfather and her father less than three feet away in her album, but suddenly it didn't feel like enough. She wanted to see that their photo was hanging on the wall of the museum, that someone remembered her family had lived there, and that their faces would be seen by whatever public happened to pass through those curated halls. She couldn't imagine who would go to Britannia Beach just to see that place, but there was no accounting for what tourists did these days. Any time she was downtown she would see groups of tourists from Asia with their cameras, and it always gave her a funny feeling she couldn't quite name.

In any case, there seemed like nothing to do but to go. The young man seemed insistent—he was doing some sort of research about it, marine biology was some sort of passion for him—and he was asking her with a tone that let her know it was something he really wanted to do, something he thought was a brilliant idea. She didn't want to beg off because of being old, or worse, to let him know that the idea made her vaguely afraid. So she capitulated, and the next thing she knew she was in that ridiculous little car, driving through North Vancouver.

The pleasant thing about being in the passenger side while driving north on the Sea to Sky Highway was that she was closest to the mountain, so she didn't have to see the precarious drop into the water they would take if Randal's foolish grandson didn't slow down.

She tried to say something about it, but he didn't listen to her; after reducing speed for a little while it would creep up again. Meanwhile he was prattling on and on at her about the heavy metals in the creek and the bay, and some quite in-depth information about wild salmon that she couldn't bring herself to care about.

Instead she let her mind drift, or rather, she let the view of the rock blur before her eyes. But then her eye caught a sign warning drivers to be cautious about road workers who might be on the highway—*Remember our families!* it said—and it brought the accident to her mind so suddenly she made a noise.

"What's that?" Michael asked her. She raised a hand and waved it slightly to indicate that it was nothing and he could go on about the fish.

She hadn't thought about that boy or the accident in a long time. Even now, she wasn't remembering the actual night it happened, but instead how this highway used to frighten and annoy her. Afterward, they had put up a big billboard that said *REMEMBER KEVIN*, and for more than a year people had brought flowers to it. She couldn't blame them for it—of course they wanted to remember their son, and safety was an issue on the single-lane highway—but it had stung her to have it thrown in her face every time she had to drive past.

The highway was larger now—they had expanded it for the Olympics a few years before—and as they approached the spot where it had happened she wondered if the sign would still be there. In fact, her heart started going faster than it should have, and she found she couldn't concentrate on what Michael was saying, not at all, even when she tried.

Then, faster than she'd imagined, they were past the spot. And the sign was gone. It had been more than thirty years, she supposed, or else they hadn't wanted to leave something so grisly there for all those international athletes to see—they were always whitewashing things for foreigners, she knew.

Before she knew it, they were there, not that she ever would have known that, had it not been for the signs telling her so. There was nothing about it she recognized—not at first. Just the smell in the air and a certain prickling feeling at the base of her neck.

The museum Michael had been talking about was now the main feature of the town, so far as she could tell. It was what you could see from the highway, anyway, a tiered structure of metal and glass that the light shimmered off of, as though it were a waterfall cascading down the rock face. It looked too modern to her and entirely out of place. There was something too slick about it, too smooth.

"Shall we go in?" he asked her.

Now that she was here, she felt strongly that she didn't want to go in. She didn't want to see what they had made of it, the way everything would be reduced to little blocks of text in both official languages. She didn't want to see her memories minimized and codified and indexed.

"You go on ahead," she said. "I'll catch up with you in a bit."

"Are you sure?" He looked worried, the dear thing.

"I'll be just fine. I just want to breathe in this air."

That seemed to convince him; he smiled at her and went inside. She stood there for a while, breathing the air like she'd said she would. It was fresher than in the city, definitely. But it seemed to her there was something missing from it, something she remembered. Woodsmoke, maybe, from chimneys? Something from the mine?

She walked out of the parking lot with no real thought as to where she was going. He'd told her as they were parking that the town had three hundred people still living in it, and she wondered if there was anyone she knew. She didn't trust her own powers of memory to match faces with names, especially after all this time. But the body memories were different; the way a path wound up a mountain, the way to put one foot in front of the other—these things were the same.

Before long she had found one of the paths she used to take as a girl. Her progress was slow, but not decrepit—she kept herself in good enough shape that she could walk at a reasonable pace. She remembered now, the way this path lead past a ventilation shaft connected to the mine. And from there it was maybe a fifteen-minute walk to where their house had been. She had no idea if it was still there now.

She reached the entrance of the mine and sat down on a rock a short distance away. She could look into the black and imagine the labyrinthine depths beneath her, which the men in her family had walked. As she stared, she seemed to hear footsteps, faint and shuffling. There was the breeze, and the birds, and a faint howling as the wind passed over the mouth of the hole, but also these dragging, irregular footsteps.

And before long she could see it, and as soon as she saw it, she knew what it was.

Every man she'd ever seen go down into that mine had come out different. Duller. A little less there, more hollow somehow. It had taken her father slowly, piece by piece, day by day, and it had taken her brother Mark all at once. Mark! She hadn't thought of him in so long now, and for a second his face floated up in her mind. He'd had freckles, she remembered, which none of the rest of them had. And his laugh had been musical and bright. Randal had gotten away from the mine by his own merits, and Francis had run away from them, and James had stayed to be consumed bit by bit, just like their father. As though they traded a little piece of their spirit for their wages each day.

But this thing … it was so pale it shone. It was white, like moonlight, with patches of verdigris hanging off it, wet and dripping. It scrabbled its tuber feet up and along the path, slowly coming toward her. It was more tumour than man, bulbous and hideous and rolling in on itself in folds. Its eyes were the only dark thing, blacker and deeper than the pit it had crawled out of. Those eyes grabbed hers, they drew her and pulled her in, until she felt she was no longer sitting on a rock but falling, silent and angry, amazed, falling downward without end into the fathomless depths, until she was nothing but a thing holding on, a desperate, climbing, clinging thing, trying to get back to something better, though it knew not what.

STRIKE ANYWHERE

VAUGHN SAT DOWN with a calendar to try to figure out when it had started—the exact first day that he hadn't left the house. There had been a doctor's appointment in March, he was sure, a checkup for Clara—everything was fine—which he would have marked on the calendar in the kitchen, in the upper-right corner of the square, as was his way, which he had learned from his mother, though none of his other siblings did this. March 18. He flipped back through the months, barely noticing the black-and-white photographs of vintage motorcycles. The calendar was from Barry. Barry, who always made the mistake of buying Vaughn things that only he himself would like: Barry liked motorcycles; Vaughn couldn't care less. It had taken the first few years of their relationship for Vaughn to accept that this wasn't selfishness or lack of caring, or even lack of knowledge—just a failure of imagination. Barry would have been standing in the store, knowing he was going to buy a calendar for Vaughn—on its own a good gift, something Vaughn needed and would appreciate, as he had one in every room and was always planning and checking and writing things down—but then Barry would simply have picked the motorcycle one because it appealed to him and thus was obviously the best, most desirable one. Maybe it was a failure of empathy, in the end. Barry had a hard time predicting or understanding how other people felt. He certainly didn't understand Vaughn's new phobia, his utter inability to leave the house.

Which appeared to have started in late March. The eighteenth was the doctor's, bundling little Clara into the car seat, keeping her calm in the noisy waiting room, asking the doctor a litany of questions that all seemed to have the same answer: She was fine, typical, healthy, developing normally, adorable, absolutely and completely fine.

After the doctor's, had he left the house again? For groceries? For a paper? For coffee with a friend? He couldn't remember. And for some reason it was driving him crazy—*more* crazy, he thought, was probably more accurate—not to know exactly when it had all begun.

Sometimes, when Clara was napping, he would open the front door and stare out at the street. He'd taken art classes in college, learned about perspective, how there was a vanishing point on each horizon, a place where all lines converged and infinity and nothingness became the same. The vanishing point was like a black hole, sucking in everything, even light.

This is what he saw when he looked down the street: all the houses the same, all the cars the same, getting smaller and smaller. He actually felt it that way; the house two down from his was smaller than the one next door. The Jenkinses, they were short, he knew that about them. The people at the end of the street were dwarfs, then, had to be—and the people beyond that, impossibly small Lilliputians.

He knew it wasn't really true, that if he moved from his home and walked down the street, his perception would change. But since he never left, he caught himself thinking they really were that small. Why should he leave the one place in the world that was his, that he knew was the proper and perfect size? Let the rest of the world shrink away to its vanishing points and disappear.

Clara's size seemed to change every day. She'd been six weeks old when they'd adopted her on January 28. Vaughn thought of that as her birthday, even though she'd been born in December of the year before. It was hard to believe they had gone all the way to Romania to get her, and now Vaughn couldn't bring himself to go to the end of the driveway.

Her needs were so simple to meet, and they were everything to him. Sometimes she would fuss slightly, sleeping in his arms, and he would slip the tip of his pinky finger into her mouth. She would suck instantly, her mouth working and her hard gums pressing against him with surprising force, lips sealed. When they were like that, he wouldn't think about anything at all for hours at a time.

Whenever Barry left, Vaughn was afraid he would never come back. It felt like a giant switch inside him that flipped from one anxious extreme to another. While Barry was away, Vaughn rubbed his fingers together like dry sticks and imagined all the terrible things that could happen to Barry: car accidents, mostly, sometimes involving the very motorcycles from the calendar, even though Barry didn't own one, but also roofs collapsing and escalator accidents and all manner of different shootings—psychotic lone gunman and maladjusted crazed students on rampages and gang warfare infiltrating the suburbs and cops-and-robbers shootouts. You could never predict the path of a stray bullet. But then, with cops-and-robbers shootouts there were also cops-and-robbers car chases, which brought him back to vehicular deaths. Other than bodily harm to Barry, he now had a more recent, more surprising, and somehow more upsetting worry: He worried about who Barry might run into, what he'd tell them about Vaughn (and Clara), what they'd say back to him, who might be comforting him through what surely had to be a difficult time.

But whenever Barry walked back through the door with his plodding gait and that stupid bowler hat he had worn all the way to Bucharest, the switch flipped in Vaughn's mind: After a few minutes of euphoric relief he started to worry instead about what Barry was thinking and what might upset him and what each of his reactions meant, and also when Barry would leave again, and why, and also whether he loved Clara as much as Vaughn loved Clara, and if Barry loved Clara more than he loved Vaughn, and whether love could ever be measured or quantified in any way at all.

The days had a steady rhythm. Daylight came and went, meals were made and eaten, laundry was done and undone with startling speed. Barry left and came back. Over several weeks it became clear he left more than he came back. Vaughn first thought he was imagining this, but when his suspicion burned too brightly he started keeping track of Barry's comings and goings in a ledger. He found it was true that Barry's time away was increasing, and therefore also increasing the time Vaughn spent worried. More and more often, Barry came back with something—a flat of bottled water or a couple extra bags of canned goods or reams of toilet paper and paper towels. Vaughn knew it meant something bad was going to happen, but he didn't say anything, because the sight of all these things coming into the house actually filled him with a sense of security and made him feel a weird thrill. A small part of him wondered if maybe Barry was filling up the house with everything the two of them and Clara would ever need, so that no one would ever have to leave again.

"You can't blame me for going," Barry said. "I'm not abandoning you, Vaughn, not really. I just can't live here. You have to realize that your behaviour affects me too."

The whole time he said it he had his eyes to the side, looking at Clara, who was eating Cheerios off the floor, which Vaughn was sure he'd cleaned but was still partially worrying about, even while he was trying to listen. Vaughn didn't like that Barry was leaving, but he was already used to it. He figured that he and Clara would be okay—you could get almost anything delivered if you ordered it online—but what about Barry, out there all the time, facing all those dangers? How would Vaughn ever know that Barry was okay if he stopped coming back? He imagined Barry getting smaller and smaller as he drove down the street—maybe he would drive so far he would simply become microscopic and disappear.

For Vaughn it happened in a slow cascade of moments: the wave, the look in Barry's eyes, the way the vertical strip of light from outside shrank thinner and thinner as the door closed, the sound of the latch clicking into place, the key going in, the deadbolt turning, the key sliding out, footsteps going farther and farther away, until there was nothing. Nothing but the house and Clara.

There was still Clara. Who needed changing. Who needed everything.

Which Vaughn could give her.

"You can't keep her in there with you," Barry said. He'd brought crocuses, his favourite flower, which Vaughn could never stand. "It's not healthy for her to live with someone so anxious. What kind of behaviour patterns do you think you're modelling for her?"

"She's a baby," Vaughn said. "Right now all I need to model are basic motor skills."

As if Barry would be a better father: on his own, with his selfishness and his inability to anticipate needs. Clara had been Vaughn's idea, not Barry's, and he was livid that Barry would try to take her from him now.

Vaughn needed to prove Barry was wrong, wrong to go and wrong about taking Clara. Vaughn needed a solution, needed a way to prove he could leave the house, if need be. Because he knew he could if he put his mind to it, if he saw an infallibly logical reason to. Failing that—he had to face the fact he had more or less already failed—he would simply have to trick himself.

That idea sparked something in him. He would convince himself of some danger in the house, something lurking and evil, and let that impel him and Clara outside. Then he would show Barry how normal he was—take Clara to the park and snap a couple of pictures—and when it got to be too much he would just go back home, knowing the danger was something he'd made up and not a real threat.

Not today, of course. No point in rushing things. Clara would be up from her nap soon, and expecting her snack and time in the playpen. She could pull herself up and stand now, and she did it every afternoon.

He didn't want to upset her routine.

Vaughn was surprised to find how easily he could discount his invented threats, while the ones outside of the house multiplied and grew, unrelenting in their terrible destructive potency. He tried to tell himself there was an intruder in the basement, some drifter who had pried open a window and crawled in there, murderous and hungry. But when he'd actually bundled Clara up in her powder-blue jacket and packed the diaper bag full of snacks and everything they would need, the man in the basement seemed silly. It was far more likely that a band of teens would mug him on his way to the park, or that a ring of child smugglers would have a scout there, waiting to inject him with some paralytic and snatch Clara and sell her on the black market. He would rather face one man in the basement—who was probably weak from hunger anyway—than the vicious hordes that were surely waiting outside.

He came up with more elaborate in-house dangers—he even went so far as to imagine booby traps set up around the house: a spring-loaded bed of nails that would crush him if he opened the wrong cupboard, hair-triggered trap doors to shark-infested water tanks, slip knots and nooses hidden even in the kitchen twine and dental floss.

But he would always elude them, hopping over imaginary tripwires as easily as stepping over a squeaky board. He conjured not just intruders but monsters and otherworldly creatures, invasions by his tiny neighbours, but nothing ever trumped the danger of the outside.

One day a letter arrived from Barry. Only it wasn't actually from Barry—it was from a lawyer representing Barry, contesting custody, alleging that Vaughn was unfit to take care of their infant daughter. Vaughn did not feel frightened by the letter; he felt angry. And there was such a power to that feeling, and such relief in feeling something other than worry, that Vaughn took to reading the letter over and over again in the subsequent weeks. He took to feeling the heavy cardstock in his hand, tracing the crest on the letterhead with his finger.

It was a tricky situation—if he didn't leave the house to show up at the hearing, they could take Clara away. If he could leave the house to go to the hearing, they'd have no reason to take her away.

On the day of the hearing, Vaughn dressed in his best suit. After breakfast and before her nap, he dressed Clara in her lace baptismal gown, which was so shapeless it still fit her fine. She fell asleep without fussing too much, allowing him to fasten his cufflinks and tie his tie, even polish his shoes before using a shoehorn to put them on.

The scrape of the match head and its tiny explosion sounded to Vaughn like distant applause. The lawyer's letter seemed to silently welcome the flame. He set it down on the sill and the fire leapt up the curtains far faster than he had imagined it would, fast enough to make his heart thud hard against his chest. He was worried his panic would wake up Clara, but she was still sleeping, and the fire was remarkably quiet, almost purring. The stucco on the ceiling was already turning black with the smoke.

He'd done it. Now the house was unquestionably more dangerous than anything waiting outside.

Vaughn backed up, and sat down beside the bag he'd packed with everything he wanted to keep. Clara was mercifully somehow still asleep. He would go in a second. The fire was just so interesting to watch. He wondered when Clara would wake up.

When she did, they'd leave.

A COMPLETE INDEX OF HOW OUR FAMILY WAS FORMED

after Matt Bell

A.

Addiction, a state both permanent and temporary, depending who you are and who you ask.

Adopt, to choose to take up, follow, or use. We adopted several strategies for appearing like good potential parents.

Adopt, to legally take another's child and bring it up as one's own.

Adoption, though we always hated the word.

Again, as in, "Are you going to try again?" As though the answer were simple.

Agony, wailing on the floor like animals after your birth mother took you back.

Ambulances that take too long to get to the scene of the crash.

Answering machine, an outdated term some of us still use to mean voice mail, a missed call somehow saved and listened to over and over: my brother's voice, telling me his wife has not survived their accident, failing to tell me his own life is still in danger.

Aphorism, from a cruel politician, one my dad repeated over and over, which I couldn't get out of my head: "Two blokes and a cocker spaniel don't make a family."

Autopsy, as an attempt to figure out why someone died in the manner they did.

B.

Baby. *B* is for baby, always. In every book, in every heart, with every beat. Not ball, not boy—those are both contained within the concept of baby. Baby is what *B* is for, what we were for, what marriage was for. Baby.

Baby books, countless, strewn all over.

Baby clothes, likewise strewn.

Baby shoes, worn by her but never handed down.

Birth, that mystery, which we were invited to witness for our daughter, not knowing then that she wouldn't be ours for long.

Birth mother, the only mother for our daughter, since both of us are men.

Birth mother, the powerful thing we could never aspire to be. The one with all the rights.

Brother, daughter, dog, husband, sister-in-law, two sons: none of these truly mine, and yet together we make a family.

Brother, maimed. His wife was driving and was killed on impact. His wife, whom I had never liked, who discouraged him from visiting me. My brother lost both of his legs and most of his right arm, but his left arm clung to his young son as they waited for help to get there. The paramedics had to peel his fingers back one by one to get him to let go.

Brother, memory of: Once, my brother and I dug a huge pit in the field behind our house, and he convinced me to throw all of our teddy bears and dolls into the hole. He made me cover them back up with dirt, and he wouldn't help me do it. He just watched, smirking. He said it would make us men, and there was nothing I wanted to be more.

Bruises so black I couldn't recognize his face, couldn't quite believe that it was him.

C.

Call Me by Your Name, our first date. I loved it because I hadn't read the book, and he hated it because he had.

Camera, ever present, to document every moment of our daughter's life for the fourteen days we had her. It seemed like so many pictures at the time, too many, but after she was gone it felt like we would never have enough, didn't document enough, didn't do enough of something.

Car accident, the fastest way to explain how our nephew became our son.

Control, and the loss of it.

Cruising, a holdover from our former lives, something we suspect each other of when one of us takes up running, or walking at night, or cutting through a park that seems like it could have been avoided.

Crying, ours, usually done alone, occasionally together, after losses, at happy times, and frequently from exhaustion.

Crying, our children's, something to be guarded against, to be dealt with, to be eliminated as quickly as possible.

Cursed, as a possible explanation for why we lost our daughter.

D.

Death, as tragedy, but not for us, or at least not completely, and all the guilt that comes with.

Death, by accident, or by one's own hand.

Death, inevitably.

Dentist visits, trying to figure out when we should take them, googling the recommended ages: "as soon as you see the first tooth and never wait past their first birthday." Realizing we had waited too long, and all the guilt that comes with.

Diapers, my brother's, after the accident, one of the many reasons he listed when he did the most terrible thing.

Diapers, our daughter's, so tiny, some still sitting unused in a half-empty box.

Diapers, our son's, hundreds of them, changed over and over and over again.

Do not.

Do not believe everything you hear, especially from your kids.

Do not cheat on your husband, no matter how tempting it gets.

Do not get your hopes up.

Do not wear effeminate or loud clothes, especially around the other parents, especially if both of you are going to be there, especially if it could embarrass your kids.

Drudgery, as a kind of ecstasy: Things may be boring but that means everyone is okay.

E.

Early mornings, getting kids up and out the door to school.

Early mornings, getting to work.

Early mornings, going to practices.

Early mornings, on vacation, watching my brother's son pour milk into cereal for my husband's son, and getting to call both of these boys my own.

F.

Family, as in husband and dog and daughter and sons and me.

Family, as something ever changing, something I want to be ever expanding but which can shrink as suddenly as it grows.

Family, as something formed despite external forces and systemic prejudice.

Fate, as something to make us keep going, keep trying.

Father, questions for: I thought I had given up caring what my father thought of me, but I wonder all the time what he would have made of me raising my brother's son and these other children. Whether he would have accepted my blended brood or stubbornly refused to love any one of us. I wonder what he would have thought as my skin wrinkles and my hair thins and I stoop, looking more like him every day. I wonder if there was anything I could have done to make him love me as I am.

Father, sense of self: None of my children have been biologically mine. Not my daughter, whom we will not erase from our family history despite the brevity of the time she spent in it; not my nephew, obviously, though in his case at least we share some DNA; and not my son, who my husband physically created but is so completely ours. To be a father as something I do, actions I take day after day for my children.

Fathering, a verb, a series of actions, never ceasing.

Fire, to sit around for warmth, to roast marshmallows on, to tell stories around, to show willing, eager faces how to build and light.

Forgetting, forbidden and impossible, something we vow never to do after we hand her swaddled to the social worker.

Forgetting, slow and inevitable, as she becomes reduced to photos that are harder and harder to find as years of newer photos pile on top.

Fret, to be constantly or visibly worried or anxious, as only a parent can be.

Fret, to gradually wear away by rubbing or gnawing, like our daughter on her teether.

G.

Guardian angels, praying they exist, willing them to exist and be ever in our service.

Guilt, over everything, every tear each child cries, everything we did wrong, everything we didn't do right, didn't do soon enough, or did too early. Guilt for everything we do and don't as parents, for everything we do and don't do for each other. Guilt for how we treat ourselves.

H.

Hair, neither of us losing ours, our boys growing it as they turned into men.

Hair, armpit, one son trims it, one son doesn't.

Hair, body, on legs and arms and chests and stomachs and backs and shoulders, shedding itself on every surface of the house.

Hair, facial, four men shaving in two sinks for all those years, stubble in every crack and crevice of the bathroom.

Hair, pubic, our son's, found in places it never should have been, like the mayonnaise jar.

Her, the one they gave us to love and then took back.

Her, the one who has been gone for so long, who is someone else now who does not know us and never will, though we still yearn for her. It still hurts; we still cry about her sometimes when the boys are away.

History, heterosexist and patriarchal: This is not just us, not just we two men who chose to marry and dedicate our lives to raising kids. This is queer men and women and non-binary people and trans people doing something we've always been told we can't do. This is a whole generation of families that look different but have the same pillar of love at their core. This is history in the making. This is history as an ineluctable wave of progress.

History, of a movement, of a series of movements.

History, political and personal.

History, the right side of, which we are often congratulated for being on.
Hospital, the place she was born, the place we had to go to give her back.

I.

I, singular but never alone.
I, with them, am a family.
Identity, as in, "How do you identify? And your partner?"
Identity, as in, "We don't want our child exposed to your identity."
If, if they say yes, if we can keep her, if my brother dies, if we could earn just a little more, if you really want to, if you need to have your own, if it's the only way, if you never do it again, if I can stay.
Index, as figuring out how you became what you are.
Index, as illumination, as light bulbs on a string, lighting a life.
Index, as a means of demonstrating love and loss.
Index, as terror, as in all the things that could still go wrong.
Insurance policy, my brother's, which lets us prove to the government that we can afford to raise my nephew, which gives us the money we need when my husband wants to conceive, which helps us buy our house. The insurance policy that turned my brother's accident into something positive, at least for us.
Insurance policy, mine, from which my sons will profit, with which I hope to turn my death into something positive, at least for them.
Intimacy, emotional.
Intimacy, physical.
Intimacy, sexual.

Intimacy, unreachable and untenable but somehow unavoidable, somehow always growing one arm as another withers away, like a strange sea creature of feeling that cannot keep its form against the gravity of adult life.

J.

Jackets, for team sports, for formals and weddings and sometimes funerals, jackets shoved into unwilling hands from September through to April, jackets proffered by adult men, jackets refused by boys who thought they were adult men.

Jerking off, my husband, into a cup to make our son, and often in the shower, and sometimes in places he shouldn't have.

Jerking off, my two sons, everywhere and all the time, barely hiding it sometimes.

Jerking off, privately, sometimes even when my husband was home, because sometimes it was the only thing I had for myself, and because it didn't involve anyone's pleasure other than my own.

K.

Knife, brought to school against the rules, the first suspension.

L.

List, of ways our biology has failed us, left us incomplete, not giving either one of us a womb.

Loss, of limbs, leading to a loss of will to live, a lesson my brother taught me all too well.

Love, familial.

Love, filial.

Love, marital.

Love, parental.

Love, paternal.

Luck, because good and bad are matters of perception, but luck is very real.

M.

Madness. All love is madness, but not all madness is love.

Medically assisted suicide, an outdated way to say it, and not quite accurate in my brother's case.

Memory, that crutch.

Memory, that temptress.

Memory, vicious, remembering the wrong moments and the wrong babies, bringing back the worst things about my brother after he was gone, erasing my daughter's face a little each day, sometimes abandoning me all together.

Memory: When my brother was a boy, our mother gave him a St. Christopher's medallion. When she placed it around his neck, she told him it would protect him, that it would keep him safe from accidents, from accidental death. He wasn't wearing it when his distracted wife plowed their family into a concrete barrier, and I always wondered whether it would have somehow stopped the crash. One can argue it was the accident that killed him, in the end.

Ministry, of Children, Community and Social Services, friends and then adversaries.

Mood disorder, my own, tricky to treat within a family, within a marriage, where opinions may vary on what constitutes disordered behaviour.

Morphine, four times a lethal dose of it, shot into my brother's broken body by some sympathetic angel we never could track down, freeing him of us, according to wishes he wrote out in an unusually eloquent letter.

Mother, mauled, killed at the hands of a cougar while cycling in the Rocky Mountains, something so out of character for her that neither my brother nor I could believe it when we were first given the news. Neither of us had known she was on a trip, nor that she cycled. My brother said it showed you can never really know anyone, but of that I am not sure.

Mother, memory of: She called everyone a cocksucker. It was her only swear, and she applied it across the board. When I tried to tell her once that her loving son was himself a cocksucker, she accused me of being vulgar. I could never get her to stop. This hurt me and was a failing, but of all those who have shown me how to form a family, my mother was the first.

Motives, easy to imagine but difficult to prove.

Mug shot, of our son, who looks so much like my husband, arrested for possession of drugs he of course claimed weren't his. No one more shocked than his brother, of which I was strangely proud.

My brother's dog, after the crash. He was the first member of my brother's family to become a member of mine. He paved the way, I like to think, for my nephew to come and join us. The dog was the first thing to make our home feel like his, and I will always love him for that.

Mystery, what binds our family together when so many dissolve apart.

N.

No one, what we are afraid of being if we remain unloved, unattached, not needed by anyone.
Nothing, what we are afraid of being left with in the end.

O.

Ovation, standing, at our son's first piano recital.
Overbites, corrected by braces.

P.

Parenting, a calling.
Partner, a choice.
Partners, what we call each other in public, "husbands" what we call each other around our friends. Always figuring out what to call ourselves to make everyone else more comfortable.
Phones ringing, phones answered, phones cracked and lost and broken, unlocked without permission by curious brothers and once a father, though I won't say which one.
Photographs, after the accident, all that broken glass.
Photographs, displayed around the house: haircuts and awkward growth phases and prom dates and high school graduations.
Photographs, of my brother, dead by something like his own hand, even if it wasn't his left hand, the one left to him, that held the needle.
Photographs, of my daughter's mother, smiling and pregnant and so sure she wanted us to raise her daughter.

Photographs, of my daughter's smile, an hour before we brought her back.

Photographs, of my husband's face, my favourites always the ones from before he met me, because they are the most inscrutable to me.

Photographs, of my son's baby teeth, hidden under pillows.

Photographs, of our family of three, assuming you count the dog, and then of four, and then of five. There is no consistent way to count how many people are in our family photographs now. We congregate and gather and cluster, and the boundaries are always changing.

Photographs, of potential children, like some kind of futuristic miracle, scrolling through websites and agencies looking for someone who would be ours.

Pings, on the iPad, while waiting for news of a son.

Poison, a constant danger, first avoiding giving the dog chocolate by accident, then checking every label and food for allergens and preservatives and cancer-causing dyes, then worrying about alcohol and the drugs our son "possessed."

Police, like no pride in policing, or no police at Pride. No one proud when our son calls us from the police station, no one even able to say a word.

Possession, the state of having, owning, or controlling something—never one's children.

Possession, an item of property, something belonging to someone, but not the way a child belongs to a parent.

Possession, the state of being controlled by a demon or spirit, or in a parent's case, their child. I am possessed by both my children, uncontrollably and unwillingly and completely.

Prevention, an ounce of which is worth a pound of cure.

— Q. —

Queerness, as an agenda.

Queerness, as an identity, and whether this is something we automatically pass to our sons, no matter their orientations, whether they consent to this, whether we even count as queer anymore when what we are doing seems so normal.

Queerness, as a target.

— R. —

Revocation, the legal term for when a mother changes her mind about an adoption.

Revoke, to put an end to the validity or operation of a decree, decision, or promise.

Risk, there are always risks: The family I have formed consists of individuals with bodies that are vulnerable and mortal, and the world is full of danger and peril. Risk, knowing that your happiness is bound to the fragile lives of others.

— S. —

Search party, sent out for my brother's son, when he dropped his compass and got lost in the woods behind our campsite. Blessed search party, bringing him back embarrassed and silent and sore from crying but utterly all right.

Sentence, not as a grammatical term but as delivered by a judge, to revoke an adoption licence or to cause a sixteen-year-old in possession of an illegal substance to months of community service and a counselling program.

Sister, questions about: We wanted them both to know about her. We had promised each other that she was part of our forever family, that we would remember her forever. We wanted the boys to know her. We showed them pictures, we told them stories, we did everything we could. But she was never real to them; they never really understood.

Sister, thoughts of: My brother's son, also my son, would tell me that he thought of her, his sister, all the time. That he tried to imagine her when he was little, but in his mind she was always just a Cabbage Patch Kid or a Barbie or sometimes a little blue troll named Sue. That as he grew, his imaginary sister grew with him, that he started to talk to a little girl who wasn't real, that he told kids in his class he had a secret sister they could never meet. That when he was a teenager he would fantasize about his imaginary sister sexually, that when he was in his twenties he went to a therapist to talk about it. He told me all this when he was a man in his forties, and it was the most surprising thing I'd ever heard.

Sometimes I wonder what would have happened if my brother hadn't been in the car that day, if he hadn't had to face that insurmountable challenge of recovery and find himself not up to the task. I wonder how long my husband would have stayed with me after we had to give our daughter back, before this other tragedy took our focus and attention and gave us our first son.

Sound, of a baby's breathing while asleep.

Sound, of a brother defending a brother, despite not sharing genes.

Sound, of car brakes, applied far too late.

Sound, of a confession whispered across a pillow in a marital bed.

Sound, of a grandmother's laugh as she sees her granddaughter reunited with her child.

Sound, of a knife placed on a principal's desk like a gavel.

Sound, of a son crying and crying when the dog finally had to say goodbye.

Sound, of a son saying he has to move across the country for his job, but it's a really good job, and he'll visit all the time, he swears, even as we all know he won't visit as often as we'd like.

Sound, of a woman telling you she loves your son and that he's asked her to be his wife.

Stimulation, intellectual, which one will never be as starved of as when parenting an infant.

Stimulation, sexual, which can come unbidden and at the worst possible times, which can betray you or save you on the same day, which feels like a foreign country to which you do not have a visa for whole years at a time.

Survivor, watched as a family, the four of us piled on the couch with popcorn, arguing about who should win.

— T. —

Tattoo, of my first son's first initial, behind my left ear.

Tattoo, of my second son's first initial, behind my right ear.
Tattoos, forbidden until they are at least sixteen, though one son gets one in secret at fourteen.

U.

Understanding, as currency, as necessity, unspoken.

V.

Vengeful thoughts, unwanted and unwelcome, toward my daughter's birth mother.

W.

We are pleased to inform you.
We regret to inform you.
What it takes to defend your family.
What it takes to help any one of them through anything, the minimum I must offer.
What it takes to know your son will leave you and love him anyway.
What it takes to salve the wound.
What it takes to take back what is yours.
Why, as in, "Why not?"
Wound, as a verb, as a noun, as something emotional, as something physical. Wound as family, and family as wound.

X.

X, drawn with a stick in the sandbox to show where the boys buried their treasure.

X, as in Gen X, generation of my heart, but not my husband's or my sons'.

X, what my life would have been if I had pressed it instead of the check mark on the app that introduced me to my husband.

X, the chromosome all humans share.

X, which stands for absolutely anyone, because families are made and lived through actions, so anyone can be included in the family if the family takes them in.

— Y.

Y, the chromosome we all share, but she did not.

You. You, you, and you. You my men, you my family, you my heart. You, whom everything is for, and always has been, and always will be.

— Z.

Zero, my brother's dog's name.

Zero, my husband's blood alcohol level for more than ten years.

Zero, our son's mark on his first algebra test, even though we helped him study.

Zero, the number of fucks I give about what anyone thinks of me, or my husband, or our sons, or our daughter, or the lifestyle we lead.

FEELINGS AND HOW TO FEEL THEM

I CAN'T SLEEP.

Which is something that used to happen to my father all the time, and how gross is that, to end up just like your dad? Maybe if I had been the kind of son who always wanted to be just like him, the paterfamilias, maybe then I would be happy? Like, "Wow, great, I did it! Now I *too* have dorky old T-shirts for pyjamas and threadbare underwear with questionable elasticization in the waist and fallen arches and insomnia!" Are there men who think like that? I doubt it, and if they did, then they would be happy and able to sleep, each of them out like the proverbial and literal light (and not like their poor insomniac fathers after all, if you stop to consider it), and I would probably *still* be sitting here awake, exhausted, and stuck with repetitive thoughts.

I keep going over all the things that happened today, trying to figure out when I could have reacted differently, or else mitigated or managed my reactions or whatever, so that maybe I wouldn't have ended up alone in bed, with Jack snoring on the couch in the living room—which somehow sounds louder than when he's actually in bed beside me, by the way—and my daughter out of the house, God only knows where, doing who knows what.

I mean it's not like I think she's dead or anything—just to be clear, my anxiety hasn't gotten that bad—but I do think in the context of the events of today that she should be here under her own roof, and we should have had a conversation, *as a family*, about that thing she was wearing around her neck for one, and about the behaviour she and her friends displayed earlier this afternoon for another. And about respect. And I think that her absence under this roof right now is not something that should be allowed and definitely not, well, *snored* through.

So anyway I couldn't sleep and I was just thinking about everything over and over again, so I thought I would try that practice I read about in *Feelings and How to Feel Them* where you write down your thoughts in order to purge them from your mind so that they lose their power over you, or you gain power over them or whatever so you can fucking go back to sleep, is the point. So here I am, my skin looking saggy and sort of older than I had realized and such a weird pale colour in this ghostly blue-white screen light, and I'm clacking away on this non-ergonomic keyboard hoping any of this makes sense.

Except now I'm realizing I'm actually kind of hungry, and maybe that's why I can't sleep.

Okay, so I got myself a snack, and to do so I had to sneak by Jack on the couch. And when I say sneak it's really just the idea of sneaking, like in my mind I did these big cartoonish steps with high knees, and there was somehow a soundtrack of a descending minor scale while I walked down the stairs, and little tinkling noises as I inched by, which I guess just goes to show that television really does rot your brain and sort of give you an indelible and fixed impression about things when you are too young to know better, and it made me wish we had paid more attention to what Ethel has been watching her entire life up until now. But anyway in reality I sort of scuffed my slippers a bit and tried to slam the fridge (it's hard because of those rubber strips, the best you get is all the jars and bottles on the door shifting and clinking, but by that point the door is already closed and it's all muffled and unsatisfying), because if I'm being truly honest with myself, which is supposed to be the point of this typing-out-your-feelings thing, like it's supposed to be all confidential so you can write freely as though no one will ever read it, and you can even erase it if you want to, but I can already tell that I will probably want to keep this and maybe even read over it tomorrow, maybe even first thing when I get up, just so my most honest emotions are fresh in my mind as I go about the new day—a new day that can turn out any way I want it to if I just vibrate on the right level or whatever. So I feel like I'm going to save it, but I have to come up with a filename that Ethel would never look at, and maybe try to make it password protected if I can figure that out, and make sure the password is something she would never guess. Because even though she has her own computer now and stuff, she did go through that really snoopy phase a couple years ago when she was fourteen and I just wouldn't ever want her reading this.

Anyway the whole point I'm trying to get to is that if I'm really honest with myself, I was kind of hoping Jack would wake up, because I really did want to talk to him more in depth about everything that happened today, like tell him the rest of what happened, and plus why should I be the only one who's up all night, worried? But of course he just slept through my whole snack, even with my slipper shuffling and fridge semi-slamming and clinking the knife on the plate kind of hard when I was slicing my sandwich in half. He hates it when I cut them on the plate and not the cutting board, which I did on purpose for the noise and so that he would be even more pissed off when he woke up, but it also made me sort of glad he didn't. But only a bit.

Okay so I guess the crux of what happened—I guess I should start in the middle, isn't that a thing, from Milton or whoever? Not that I think my day is an epic poem or anything, but I'm not going to lie, it did feel kind of epic, at least to me.

So basically the whole thing is that we woke up to mega snow, and so of course Jack and I put on the television to see if schools were cancelled, and in that way things go the high schools were telling kids to stay home, but the colleges were open, so Jack was going to have to drag his ass in and teach and Ethel was going to be home all day, which basically already meant that I wasn't going to get anything done with my sculpting or probably even the cleaning. Okay whatever, at first it was just a lot of little things, like Jack was really crabby at me even though nothing about the situation was remotely my fault, and then I went in to tell Ethel we'd seen on the local news that her school was cancelled, and she literally made this annoyed sighing sound and said, "I know, dad, I saw it on Insta like so long ago when I first woke up, now I'm trying to go back to sleep." And she didn't sound excited about her day off or spending the day with her dear old dad, not at all. And I swear she basically rolled her eyes at me, even though they were closed.

So yadda yadda yadda, Jack goes off to work in his stupid huff or whatever—I just don't get why he can't make more of an effort to sort of be conscious about his affect, you know? Because that kind of thing really does rub off on the people you live with, like there are all kinds of clues in posture and body language and breathing and stuff that our subconscious takes in, and it's just really easy sometimes to feel certain things are directed at you, even if the person doesn't realize it. Anyway, this is an issue in our relationship that we've been trying to work on for a long time—well at least I have—and it doesn't really have to do with today except that it all just kind of adds up.

So Jack's gone and suddenly Ethel is up and basically looks at me like, *Where's breakfast?* when here I thought she was going to sleep in for way longer and also, the times when I make her breakfast she never wants it and so of course the one time I don't make it because I'm trying to show her that I get that she is independent and a burgeoning adult who is capable of feeding herself, she gets pissed off. So basically she is eating this piece of toast in the most snarky way—I don't even know how she does it, but it was *snarky*—and then she tells me she wants to have her friends over to watch Netflix.

It always kills me how there is too much snow for them to go to school, but somehow they are fine to all make it to each other's houses.

So next thing I know there are six girls—young women—in my house. And I know them all of course and it's completely okay, and part of me is actually liking it, like in my mind I make them all cookies—the delicious smell of my baking brings them away from the cold glare of the screen and they come into the kitchen and ask if they can help and we all sort of stir bowls of batter and chat about fashion and pop stars and which celebrities are dating and then we eat warm baked goods and feel guilty but in a satisfied cheat-day, shared-secret kind of way.

So basically this line of thinking led me to really crave a chocolate chip cookie, and I was pretty sure we still had a couple bags of the President's Choice ones, so I went to go get them and I was totally going to maybe even put some on a plate and offer them to the girls. But when I walked into the living room they all kind of turned to me and acted all shy and weird, and then the Polish one from down the street whose name I always get wrong—Jolonka? Jalinka?—she nudged Ethel in this go-ahead kind of way, and Ethel says they want to ask me a question.

I thought they were going to ask if they could drink or something, which I was definitely going to say no to. Then Ethel looks at me, her own father, and says: "We were wondering if you could tell us how to give a good blow job."

What the fuck? I honest to God don't know what to say in this moment. They're all looking at me like I'm the most interesting thing they've ever seen—which is never how they look at me—and they're literally waiting with bated breath. I have this crazy fantasy of not saying anything and seeing how long it takes them to turn red and pass out from forgetting to breathe.

"'Cause, you know, we figured you must be good at it." This was from Ricki, a girl I had stopped from drinking glue on countless occasions—she had literally been hell-bent on actually drinking it, when most of the other kids at worst would spread a thin layer on their fingers and then peel it off and try to gross each other out with the "skins." I could remember prying the bottle of glue out of her hands, could remember how her pink nail polish—the same shade she was currently wearing—would always be chipped and that was what I'd stare at as I pried her surprisingly strong fingers off the glue bottle, always wondering if I was being too forceful and if there was a better way for me to communicate why drinking glue was not a good idea. The last time I took the glue from her feels like it was ten days ago, or at longest last summer, but I guess it must have been more like ten years ago. Jesus Christ.

And they're still staring at me.

I'm not really sure what my move is here. I mean don't get me wrong: I am great at giving blow jobs—more than one guy has told me I'm a genius at it—and there are definitely things I could teach these girls. And if they're going to be giving them anyway—oh my God, what if they already are?—they might as well be good at it, right? For a second I picture getting a banana from the kitchen and really getting into it. But something about the way she said it was just a hundred different kinds of wrong, not to mention what their parents would say to me if they ever found out. I could just imagine *those* conversations. The more I thought about it, the more I didn't like the way they were looking me. Suddenly I couldn't believe I had even considered teaching my daughter and her friends about the best way to pleasure a penis with their sixteen-year-old mouths.

It wasn't just that—there was something insulting about it too. Like in a nice way they were calling me a cocksucker, the same as every kid on the playground ever had.

It was then I noticed Ethel had something dangling at her neckline that she hadn't been wearing in the morning, and that at least a couple other girls were wearing one as well. It was all I needed to avoid answering their question.

"What's that around your neck?"

She looked at me as though I had called her fat. She looked at me as though I had just asked her, in front of all her friends, why she still wet the bed. She wasn't just angry, she was hurt. Or maybe scared.

And then the other thing was—I couldn't tell if this was better or worse—I hated the way my voice sounded when I asked it. I sounded just like my father.

How many times had he asked me that question? In my case it was always something he thought of as too feminine—hell, he was probably right, I was fourteen years old and in that small town and when I look back now, I can't believe I didn't get beaten up, but at the time I thought he just hated me because I wasn't manly enough, wasn't the perfect boy he'd always wanted. "What are you wearing?" he'd ask me, and I'd always be too afraid or too embarrassed to answer. I wish I'd had half the sass Ethel has. Wish I'd had the gall to say "my sister's jeans" without even stopping, then grab a piece of fruit and bite it as I walked away. God, just thinking about it now gives me goosebumps. Would Dad have belted me? Part of me thinks he would have, but he never laid a hand on us. We were afraid of him, though. We were afraid of him when we were bad. I don't know that Ethel's ever afraid of me, no matter what she's done. But maybe that's just girls?

She didn't say anything, just stared at me with that annoyed, pissed off look, but her eyes weren't shooting hate beams like they sometimes do, and the corner of her mouth was trembling, which is how I knew her feelings were actually hurt underneath. Jesus, it was easy to do that.

At these moments, I always think, *It's because she's a woman*, or *Must be the hormones*, or once, horribly, *I guess she's on the rag*. As soon as I think one of these things, I hate myself. I mean, it's misogyny, right? And I have a daughter. I can't believe I think like that. And so as soon as I think like that, I give her anything she wants. The worst part is, she knows it.

So I went over to her—because now I had to follow through—to look at the necklace that caught my eye. It was a simple leather strip, doubled or tripled around her neck, and at the bottom of it hung—well, it looked like those green plastic things that come at the bottom of fresh flowers. A vial, I guess you'd call it, except the plastic was clear, and it was filled with something liquid, and red.

"What is this?" I asked her. Again, it came out with more tone than I'd meant to use.

"None of your business, Dominic," she said. She pushed herself off the table she was sitting on and grabbed her book bag off the counter. Her friends didn't even say goodbye, they just filed out after her. Solidarity. But I thought it was rude. If it had been me, and my friend's dad had embarrassed him in front of me, I would have let my buddy walk out first and then I would have said, "Bye,

Mr. So-and-So," or "See ya," and then when I joined my friend outside we would have cut their dad to shit.

Was I a hypocrite? Was I a suck-ass? Suddenly I was glad Ethel's friends hadn't said anything to me—it meant they were good friends, better than I was to mine, and that was good. She needed that. She had people looking out for her in the world, and that was something.

I could hear them pulling on all their coats and hats and boots in the hall, not saying anything. How did they know not to break the silence? And then they all shuffled out. All I felt was a cold wind around my bare ankles.

So, I called Jack. I know his phone password, so I can go back now and hear my own messages, which is sort of pathetic but maybe is just sort of part of my process and just where I am tonight. I want to transcribe them to really sit with where I was in the moments I left them, to really mine them for emotional truths. I'm trying not to judge myself but just to really express the way I'm feeling, both earlier today and now.

"Hey, Jack." I've only said two words and already this voice mail sounds weird. I knew it when I was leaving it but I couldn't change it after. Like if I erased it I would have had to start all over. What was wrong with my voice today? "It's not an emergency or anything, but I guess I just wanted to talk—if you're free—like, if you can call me back, that would be great, but no pressure. I just had a thing with Ethel, no big deal, but she's wearing this new necklace? And it was some kind of vial and it had in it, like, this red stuff? That—well, I mean I don't know of course—I mean how would I—but it kind of looked like, blood? Maybe? And I just thought, you know—maybe we should ask her about that? Or I mean, discuss our position on it, as co-parents, and then maybe talk to her? Or I mean, we should talk about how we feel if it is blood, and then we should find out if it is blood, I guess by asking her. Anyway, I'm sure this is a lot to take in, and obviously you're busy because you didn't answer, but, you know, yeah—I guess I'm saying if you get this, give me a call."

"Jack, it's me again—ha, I guess that's obvious—but I was just wondering if you got my other message. I mean, if you got it and you were able I'm sure you would have called me, because I asked you to, so I know logically since you haven't called me, you haven't gotten it. But I know also sometimes you don't check your phone if you get caught up in a good workflow, and I know you have office hours or whatever, assuming you had to teach your classes, so I just thought if I called again maybe you would hear it ring or vibrate or whatever, unless you have it on Do Not Disturb or just totally off, even though that would basically defeat the point of having it. And I have to say in that case I would be jealous of your phone—ha, ha, get it?—because I am definitely disturbed. I mean if Ethel is carrying blood around on her neck, I just want to go ahead and open the discussion now: I am against it. Or, well, I would have a lot of feelings to process about it. Anyway, I'm getting ahead of myself—of us. So just to say, call me when you get these, which I hope is soon."

Then I tried to figure out what a good thing to do is while you wait for your husband to get home to discuss whether your teenage daughter—who may or may not be giving blow jobs, which you haven't even told him about yet—is wearing a vial of blood around her neck. One idea I have is to cut myself a little and try to bleed into one of those green plastic things you get at the end of cut flowers, just to see if it looks the same. We have a whole drawer of them from the odd time when Jack actually brings me flowers, which isn't a lot—not that I'm complaining. But I would definitely say I bring them to him more. And I mean, maybe that's how Ethel did it, assuming she did it, maybe that's the drawer she got the vial from. Then I'm thinking about how she did it—and okay, to be really honest all I can think about since I saw it is whose blood it may or may not be—and then when I'm thinking about that it occurs to me that whenever anyone wants to know how to do anything these days, they go to Google.

And so, a dilemma: Do I google whether this is a thing? Like what if I google *teenagers blood vials necklace* and I find out something truly horrible, something I am definitely not ready to handle? Like that they wear the blood of the person who took their virginity? Or the first person they gave a blow job to? Or, oh my God, what if it is some kind of ritual thing where you take the blood of all the guys you have given blow jobs to and you wear it in a vial around your neck?

Anyway I can't bring myself to do it, and cutting myself seems dumb. It's not going to prove anything. I can't remember for sure exactly what it even looked like.

"So I guess maybe you aren't calling me because you don't believe me, or something? But Jack, it *really* looked like blood. Like really. And I guess you're thinking that I don't know what blood looks like, but

I do. I mean, I've seen it. There was just—you could just tell there was nothing else it could be. Like nothing else looks like that, not grenadine, not the fake blood they use for all that zombie stuff they do, nothing. You can't fake blood. It always looks fake, but this blood didn't. It was so real. And I know real blood wouldn't stay liquid forever, right, so I'm thinking she must have added something to it? Or like, maybe there was Aspirin residue in the vial from using it for plants and that is acting like an anti-coagulant? Maybe? And Jack, I'm just wondering if you have any ideas about why she's doing this, or where she might have gotten it? I mean, is it something you two have talked about privately, or just when I'm not around? Because it's definitely something I'm very concerned about, and when you don't call me back it makes me feel as though you're not concerned about it at all, which I also find concerning. And it also makes me feel unheard. Not to problematize or escalate the situation, because I know you are in fact at work—well, hopefully commuting home from work at this point—but it's starting to bother me that I haven't heard back from you. Even a text would have been nice. Okay. I love you."

And I don't even know whether this is relevant to my feelings or my insomnia, but I should also say that in this time waiting for him to get home I made what I thought was a pretty decent dinner, because the cooking just sort of helped pass the time and helped me not to think about things, and also it is just a nice thing to do when you live with somebody.

And okay I don't want to sound petty or anything, but Jack walked in and said hi *like nothing had even happened!* I'm sorry but

I really find that strange. And I had to act sullen and quiet before he even asked me what was wrong.

"Don't you want any dinner?" I asked him, because he hadn't even said anything about the set table or the food that was out.

"I'm not that hungry," he said, which just doesn't make any sense. I still don't get that. And I had to be sort of sullen and non-responsive more, for what felt like forever, until he finally sighed in this super-annoyed way, which may or may not have been actually directed at me, and he said, "What's wrong, D?"

And I didn't really appreciate him using a cute name for me like that at such a serious time. So I said, "Did you get my messages?"

"Oh yeah, I got them," he said. "I was busy. Something about Ethel wearing blood?" He had opened the refrigerator and was looking for something to eat—was he hungry or wasn't he? Didn't he see that I had made him dinner? I mean, could he not literally see the plates that were in front of him on the table? Or did he just not care? And wait—

"Did you say you got them? My messages?"

"Don't rag on me," he said—there was that word again. "I've been teaching all day. Give me a couple minutes to adjust."

Something about that killed me—you shouldn't have to adjust to your home. It should be where you feel the most comfortable.

So after that nothing went right. It's hard for me to like, type out who said what after that, and it's all kind of a blur in my mind, but basically he just thought it was no big deal that Ethel had left without saying where she was going or checking in with us—he said he was sure she was just at one of the other girls' houses, and that they weren't going far with the storm being so bad and the roads all shut down, and that she was old enough to have a sleepover without telling us every little thing. And then *of course*, right at the peak of this, she texted *him* and said they were all staying at the Rizowskis, and he just looked at me like, *See?* And when I asked him if he wasn't worried about boys he just shrugged, and said that for all we knew she could be into girls—which is just stupid, especially knowing what I know about her curiosity around fellatio.

Which—okay—I didn't tell him about that part, because he was being so laid back about the blood necklace—like he said we would just ask her about it when she came home, and if it was blood we would say she wasn't allowed to wear it in the house. Actually he said, "If you're creeped out by it, we'll just tell her she can't wear it at home." And then we got into such a big fight.

Jack does this thing where he makes everything sounds logical and simple, and makes it seem like I am having these big over-the-top reactions to something small and insignificant. But I just don't see how you can think a vial of blood is small or insignificant. I don't know how he doesn't care more about things.

Or maybe I just mean more about me.

THINGS GIVEN, THINGS WITHHELD

1.

WHEN I FOUND OUT, when it became really real, I was at my office Christmas party. We were in the final weeks of 2003, and reams of snow had blanketed the city the night before. I remember Helen Cherrybindle from accounting suggested Jäger shots, and before that day none of us even knew she drank, which Tommy had mentioned out loud to her face.

"Girl," he said, "none of us even knew you drank."

Helen snorted and said, "I drink *at least* a bottle of wine every night. That's like my base. Just to get me through the week."

There were nods from everyone in the circle. I tried to make it look like I was agreeing without actually nodding. Because even though I also drank at least a bottle of wine every night, I wasn't quite drunk enough at this moment in time to admit it to my co-workers. I already felt guilty by association. One of these nodding people could be a mole from the higher-ups, who would go back and report our drinking patterns and say, "Everyone was talking about how they drink a bottle of wine *every* night, and Linden didn't say *anything*, which means he probably does it too."

But Helen, who had consumed four nine-ounce glasses of California Chardonnay, wasn't finished.

"And then on the weekends, I just go crazy." She stopped then, but just to look everyone in the eye with a demonically seductive smile. "You know what, guys, we should get crazy *right now*. We should do Jäger shots!"

This was greeted by cheers all around—I mean, the bar had one of those chilling machines, so you knew it was going to be *really* cold, which is the best way to have Jäger—and next thing I knew I was slamming a shot glass onto the bar, swallowing a delicious digestif made of fifty-six herbs and spices, being slapped on the back by Jaspreet from accounting, and feeling a metaphorical buzz in my brain and a literal buzz in my pocket.

When I took my phone out, the text was from Anna.

Just wanted to tell you I gave birth to a healthy baby girl. You have a daughter!

It was immediately followed by a picture of Anna looking red and sweaty, and then an even redder, sweatier face scrunched up in blanket with a little cap on its head. It was like someone had handed her a newborn monkey at the zoo.

I felt a moist palm against my back and before I knew it Tommy's reedy voice was at my ear: "Whose baby is that?"

"My cousin's," I said. I wondered if my face showed that I was lying. When I was younger I could always get away with a lie by making my face kind of blank—if you can convey a lie with an expression of utter boredom, almost everyone believes you. But now that I was in my mid-thirties and suffered from a near-constant subcutaneous anxiety about almost everything, it was hard to look so bored. I looked nervous and guilty all the time, no matter what, so everything seemed like a lie. Luckily this was good enough as cover most of the time, because no one lies as often as that either. At least no one normal.

"It's disgusting," Tommy said. He handed me a shot of Jäger that was only slightly warmer than ideal. "To hell with breeders!" he said, then cheersed me, then we both slammed one back.

As he turned away I slipped my phone out of my pocket just to make sure it wasn't on, that I hadn't accidentally butt-dialled Anna and that she hadn't accidentally heard this conversation. But everything was fine.

I might as well just go ahead and admit that I don't remember how many drinks I had that night, but the next day no one was talking about anything crazy that I did, which was a victory in its own way. Tommy had apparently thrown up at the bar and been escorted out by a bouncer, then embarrassed himself further by first asking for the bouncer's number and second getting out of the cab he'd been poured into at a distance of only a block away to puke again and then teeter back and make faces at us through the window, trying to get us to let him in through some non-existent back door. Helen had passed out and been unwakeable after last call, which was relatively mild, though embarrassing enough to make the rounds of gossip. Speaking of gossip, Simon mentioned to Carla in passing that he'd seen Deborah have a glass of wine, not knowing that Carla was one of the select few in on the secret that Deborah was pregnant with twins but trying to hide it until after they decided about her promotion. All the moms were pretty judgmental about that glass of wine, but about a third of them said one glass on occasion was totally fine, and then Deborah claimed it was non-alcoholic anyway. But Carmel had it the worst, because she hit on the VP, Jerry Godard, who was married, naturally, and who turned her down rather rudely. Her gossip was the worst because it caught the most attention of the most people the highest up, and because it threatened to ruin the fun for everybody; next year, and for maybe the next two or three years, you could bet that the office Christmas party would be on a weeknight and not a Friday or a Saturday, and/or that the number of free drinks would be limited, and/or that some other countermeasure would be taken to make sure that nights like last night never happened again.

But the pendulum swings both ways, and no matter how far into the safe zone things might swing, they always eventually start to swing back and get more lax.

2.

I might as well also admit that it was a couple of days before I texted Anna back. A few days. It was a little too long, I get that—but it was definitely under a week. The main thing was that I didn't want to disturb the baby. Like, what if she spent hours trying to get her to sleep, and then right when she was finally out—*wham!*—donor dad chooses to phone right at that moment. The baby would wake up and scream, so Anna and I wouldn't be able to have a conversation anyway, and then she would just have to spend hours getting her to sleep again. That didn't seem like very supportive behaviour on my part.

And sure, there were other things going on. With me, I mean.

3.

Suffice it to say that soon after that, I plucked up the courage to actually call Anna—baby screams be damned—and we arranged for a visit and I went out to meet the Monkey (who is named Persephone, of all the sweet and holy things), and we started to forge our strange and unique relationship for which there are so few models.

People always ask me what it felt like the first time I held my own child in my arms. And it seems like the two reactions people are most expecting is that I would either want to eat the baby or kidnap the baby. "Didn't you just want to eat her? Didn't you just want to eat her right up?" Honestly, I am surprised more babies don't die or get injured from cannibalism. "Didn't you just want to run away with her and keep her all to yourself?"

The thing is, I didn't. Anna had the good grace to hand her to me when she was clean and dry and smelled nice, although soon I would encounter her in the opposite of all three of those states. She felt warm and a little squooshy and somehow both heavier and lighter than I expected. She felt like a dozen other babies I have held before and since. It's not that it wasn't one of the most profound and amazing moments of my life—it totally was—it's just that it didn't change anything fundamental for me.

People always look disappointed when I say that, and maybe it disappoints me a little bit too. But whatever.

The point is that I visited for a week in Montreal and then I headed back to Toronto and my life went on pretty much as normal. Anna and I texted all the time like we did before and we sent each other a lot more pictures—well, she sent me a lot more pictures—and we lived essentially separate lives.

And soon after this, Helen Cherrybindle went through a nasty divorce and the two of us started spending a lot more time together out of the office.

4.

The night that ended up changing the rest of my life started just like all the ones that didn't, namely, pre-drinking at someone's house before going out on a Friday.

In this particular case it was Tommy's house—we alternated weekly between Gay Night and Ladies' Night and, when Jaspreet complained, we occasionally threw in Guys' Night. Though the general consensus when we were away from said guys was that Guys' Night is gross—it always seems to lead to either chicken wings or strippers, and in the worst cases, both.

This particular Gay Night was starting out at Tommy's, where we would drink heavily, then go out to see drag queens, which is generally what gay people in the office do with ladies and adventurous straight male co-workers. The pre-drinking in theory is a money-saving tactic, supposedly to offset the overpriced drinks at the bar. If you go in already drunk, the theory states, then there's no need to waste money on drinks once you're there.

Like most theories it's so full of holes you could drain spaghetti with it. First of all, the drinks at Talons are pretty fucking cheap. And second, going in already drunk doesn't prevent you from buying drinks; by the time you get there you're already so far in the bag that good decision making has flown fabulously out the window. I could go on, but you get the drift: These nights are a mess.

So Tommy had a roommate who punked out on the rent half-way through the month, because he took off somewhere with some guy, so Tommy had been subletting the extra room to this college student named Brad. Brad invited a bunch of his friends over. As far as I could tell their ages ranged from close to twenty to a little too far past thirty. I was wearing a tank top that for some reason said '85 on it. Which I guess made it kind of sporty—I was going for a jersey sort of thing, never mind. There was this one guy there—this is kind of embarrassing—okay he was more of a jock than I normally go for, but he was really cute and had this sort of Zac Efron hair—I know, I can't believe I know who that is either—and he just kept staring at me.

Oh, I should also say that I had brought a bottle of wine. And when I say that, I don't mean like a normal classy 750-millilitre bottle of wine. What I mean is that I brought a magnum (for those not in the know, that's a 1.5-litre bottle of wine, a.k.a. two bottles of wine in the convenience of a single glass bottle). And while I'm feeling honest I should also say that, yes, contrary to what you think the laws of physics and social graces might dictate, I drank the whole thing.

But I had nowhere near finished it when the jock kid—whose name, it turned out, actually was Zac—finally said to me, "Hey man, cool shirt."

Which okay, is not the best opener on the face of the earth, but I had to give him props—if that's still what the kids are calling it—for talking to me at all. So I said, "Thanks, you're pretty cute too." Which isn't really a quid pro quo kind of answer, but which I felt at least, you know, set the tone.

He looked kind of confused but he rolled with it and said, "Yeah, like, '85—that's the year I was born."

At which point—well, after stammering in disbelief and getting myself the hell out of there, you can believe I went straight to the fridge and fished out my magnum and did not let it leave my side for the rest of the pre-drinking portion of the night. Which somewhat—okay I get maybe not, but maybe sort of you get it—explains why I drank the whole thing.

Anyway. The point. I am getting to it. This is all foreplay, you know. I'm circling around to something deadly. It's like how a shark swims to close in on prey, but it's also the best way to play with a nipple. Or something.

The point is we all had a great time at Tommy's, and then in one gasping crush of multigenerational glory we set out to see men dress in women's clothing and lip-synch to pop songs, and it was divine. We walked up the steps and into the bar and—

—and then I woke up in my own bed, naked and alone. Which is either pathetic or impressive, depending how you look at it.

Anyway this would all be a sort of run-of-the-mill amusing blackout story if it weren't for the following chain of events.

Checking to see if I have my wallet and phone and all those good things, I crawl across the bed and reach onto the floor, where I see my jeans and socks and shirt in a crumpled pile, as though I had immolated or raptured and left my clothes behind me. I pick up my jeans and find my wallet in one pocket where it should be, and in the other, my phone, yes, but also my underwear, crumpled into a little ball. Meaning, they were off of my body and picked up by my hand (or someone else's) and shoved into the pocket of the jeans—which I was wearing—and walked home by my legs. Hunh.

Upon making this discovery I felt a dropping sensation in my stomach, a kind of yawning pit of dread, which I wanted to just be hangover-related nausea but already felt like something different. I went into the bathroom and looked at myself in the mirror, and everything seemed normal. I turned around and craned my neck to try to see my back—sending black stars and white points of light streaking across my field of vision—and then I noticed them: little bruises on several parts of my back. Not hickeys. Bruises. I didn't even know what activity—presumably between two men—could make bruises like that.

Back to the jeans, I found one more piece of evidence: a scrap of paper that said *Omar* with a phone number scrawled beside it.

Like any frightened animal, I called for help—in this case by dialling the ten digits belonging to Helen Cherrybindle. I explained the situation. My voice was shaking. I was scared. The look of those bruises freaked me out. I had no idea what had happened.

"Oh my God, that's *hilarious*," Helen said. "Don't worry, I won't tell anyone at work." Unbelievably that hadn't at all been what I was worried about, though now I added it to the list.

"But Helen," I said. "Anything could have happened."

"But you're fine. It's just a funny story."

"Anything," I said again. "*Anything*." There was only one specific thing I was talking about, but she didn't get it.

I called Tommy but he didn't answer. I spent the rest of that day in bed.

5.

All I remember about going to get results is the walk down to the clinic.

I remember that I took the stairs instead of the elevator, because the elevators in my building were just so cramped and breaking down all the time, and I was only on the fifth floor. There was someone smoking in the stairwell, which is illegal and supposed to get you evicted—he had a shaved head and sores on his arm. I remember wondering about the sores as I walked by, but now I think they were probably just from drugs.

The first thing I heard when I stepped outside was a siren. Then birds. Then that sort of background wash of voices and traffic and everything else. I suddenly wished I had asked someone to come with me, but first of all it was too late, and second of all I didn't want anyone at the office to know either way, and I didn't really have many friends from outside of work anymore. At least that's the way it felt.

I walked down the street and there was this guy standing there with a clipboard and a pen and one of those vests—I remember it as a vest, anyway—and he was soliciting for charity.

He said, "Make a donation to support the Toronto People with AIDS Foundation?" And I said, "No, thank you!" and pushed past him, because I was freaked out and nervous and in a rush.

And then immediately I thought, *Because you didn't give any money, your test will come back positive.* And I almost turned around and went back, but the voice said, *It's already too late.*

So I kept walking, the whole while telling myself that the voice was magical thinking, that reality didn't work that way, that it was a by-product of fear and anxiety, that it was ridiculous, that it wasn't true.

But of course it was.

6.

I'm visiting with Anna and the Monkey—they're just "stopping by" en route to visiting Anna's cousins in Guelph, but I have a feeling that seeing me was the real reason Anna planned this big drive. There's something strange about the way she's been looking at me, but it's probably just in my head.

"I just think a sibling is so important," she said. "Don't you?" I never answered these little questions when she dangled them; I thought they were rhetorical. Didn't she know that by now? Wasn't it obvious? And yet she would look at me until I started to talk, and then interrupt. I waited, but nothing seemed to be coming.

"Well, actually—" I said.

"Because I do. Not just for the socialization while they grow up, which is very important, but also so they'll always have someone there for them after I die." Somewhere during this speech I stared at Monkey, who really did look like her namesake.

"Do oom want a widdle brother or sister?" I cooed.

"Don't infantilize her!" Anna chided.

"She's an infant," I said. It was the truth, and it was the only defence I had to cloak myself in.

"Her brain is a sponge right now, Linden," Anna said. "A *sponge.* What if she accidentally hard-wired your cute mistakes into her brain?"

"I'm sorry," I said.

"Me too," said Anna. "I want her verbal development to be as accelerated as possible."

I wondered what would accelerate my verbal development, or whether all my development was done. Wasn't that why middle age was depressing, why people wanted to have children in the first place? To distract themselves from the fact that they themselves had stopped growing or developing in any meaningful way? Sure, there was the odd bout of mandated professional development, but that hardly counted.

"Are you even listening?"

"I'm not sure I understand the thrust of this conversation," I said. I was thinking about whether or not it would look inappropriate to pour myself a third drink. Anna hadn't had any that I'd noticed, so it was likely she was counting mine.

"Wait, you're not trying to tell me that you're ..." I thrust my eyebrows toward the general direction of her womb with what I hoped was a meaningful glance.

"Well no, doofus," she said. She was blushing, which was something I hadn't seen since—oh no. "I'm trying to ask you if you'll donate again."

It was all I could do not to slam my hands on the table and walk out, except it was my apartment. I should just tell her that it wasn't possible. Could I tell her that I'd had a vasectomy? She would never believe it. And yet I had to say something, had to do something to stop this before she got it in her head. The least disappointed she would ever be was if I just told her right now. Point-blank. Maybe not the whole truth, but at least that I couldn't donate. I had to say something.

"Well, sure, we can talk about it." Those were the words that came out of my mouth. With a pretty halting expression on my face. In fact I was pretty sure my face had turned into a giant stop sign—why couldn't she see it?

Her face crumpled into a wad of Kleenex for just a nanosecond, then bloomed out again into a visage of calm reasonability.

"Great!" It was three notes too cheery. I was supposed to have said yes right away and been excited about it. "I so enjoyed all our discussions leading up to the first time."

"Me too," I said. "All those fantastic bottles of wine." Stupid.

"I mean I'm not sure that there will be a lot of new content. Everything would be pretty much the same, just the second time around. Right?"

"Right." Except that this time I have a virus and my fluids are poison.

"Unless ..." She stops as she says this, and looks really concerned for the first time. "You're not with somebody, are you? Seeing someone that you haven't told me about? Who might have a problem with it?"

I put my hands up in front of my face. "It's nothing like that," I say. "You don't have to worry on that score." I sound like my father as I say it. My father who kept his terminal lung cancer a secret until he coughed up blood trying to blow out the candles on his birthday cake. I never ate vanilla icing again.

7.

Everyone always wants to know how we did it. Guys especially. I don't know if women are just more polite or what, but it's only guys who say, "Did you fuck her?" Almost every guy I've told has asked me that.

And no, I didn't. I take my homosexuality very seriously, thank you very much.

The rest of the people (people who give a shit, that is, most people don't really care about much beyond themselves—you can tell them you donated your kidney to your landlord's mom, or that you just gave the extra bedroom in your house to a refugee, or that you personally donated enough money to save a rare species of tiny dragon-like lizards on the other side of the world, and no one's going to actually say much about any of those things or ask any real follow-up questions, and I know this from experience)—the rest of the people assume that there were a lot of doctors and laboratories and cryogenics. They picture canisters of brushed steel and thick rubber gloves and hissing noises followed by plumes of dry ice floating down to the floor and drifting over linoleum that stretches into ominous collection rooms populated by racks of sticky porno magazines and Kleenex boxes and the lingering scent of lube. Not to mention the bills. They picture all those commas and decimals lining up, doctor's fees and storage fees and consult after consult. They wonder how much I contributed, if anything.

In actual fact we bought an over-the-counter conception aid at Rexall and it worked on our very first try. And I paid for it, not her—it felt chivalrous, or something. It comes with a little silicone cup and a wand, and I jizz into the cup and load the cup into the wand, then she inserts the wand and releases the cup. It squishes up to her cervix like getting stuck between two fat guys on the bus, and my little swimmers go where they're supposed to go, and she pulls the whole thing out like a tampon four hours later.

And then forty weeks after that, Monkey is born! A whole human being with a whole life in front of her. Who now, apparently, wants a sibling.

I'm thinking about this as I polish off a six-year-old Côtes du Rhône, and as far as I can figure out, my point—because I do have one—is that if I can get her to agree to use a clinic this time, then they will test my semen as part of all their regulations and red tape, and my sample will get flagged, and then Anna will find out that I can't be her donor again and the reason why in one fell swoop (I'll have to pretend that *I'm* just finding out, of course, but I feel reasonably confident that I can pull it off, and on the plus side it explains why I haven't told her that I'm positive in the eighteen months I've known, anyway).

But last time went so smoothly, Anna's going to want to do everything the same way again. And all the reasons we had for doing it that way the first time are going to come up again—that it just seems better to deliver the semen like bread—fresh and warm—instead of freezing it and thawing it again. And of course the financial differences are astronomical, and neither of us is exactly rolling in it—it's not like I could afford to pay for the clinics if I insisted she use them. And really everything would just take more time and be more bureaucratic and pretty much the opposite of everything Anna stands for. There's no way.

So, that means I just have to say no.

And, I tell myself, I don't have to say why. What I mean is, I can make up any reason I want. She doesn't have to know the real one.

Later, I'm riding the subway (I signed up for a yoga class but then I got halfway there and turned back). A man gets on at Castle Frank, very thin with bags under his eyes and a white beard that I would describe as scraggly, though I wonder if he thinks he looks like a wizard or something. I see him coming and adjust my hand lower on the pole so that he can put his comfortably at ninety-degree-elbow height, which is higher than mine because he's taller than me. He notices the gesture and kind of nods at me. We're looking into each other's eyes.

"Hey," I say. It's noncommittal.

"Hey," he says back.

"I'm HIV positive," I say. I'm not sure I even know I'm going to do it before it comes out. I mean, I was thinking about it, but I can't remember actually deciding to say it. I think, *I am totally without expectation in regard to his reaction,* but no sooner does that tickertape across my mind than I realize exactly what I want him to do. I want him to shrug like it's no big deal. I actually want that so badly all of a sudden that I can feel my heart preparing to race—not that the beat actually quickens, but more like a flood of some hormone or enzyme enters my blood and starts rushing toward my heart; our glands always know before our brains do.

Second place in the reaction Olympics would be if he said something sad or apologetic, if his face contorted involuntarily into some whelp of pity. And third—only because I imagine that I kind of like this guy—would be if he muttered "Me too" and shuffled his feet a bit awkwardly.

No such luck. He takes his hand off the pole, looks at it, then moves halfway down the car. A couple people watch him and try to figure out why he's looking at his hand—Did something spill, is there a gross mess somewhere?—but mostly no one looks up at all. I didn't say it loudly enough that anyone else could hear.

I'm sort of sad—I can feel that—but mostly I start trying to take things apart logically. I was just able to tell a total stranger, so obviously I am capable of telling people. The stranger's reaction wasn't ideal—it wasn't even in my top three—and that bothered me. Did it bother me?

I look down the car and see that the man has asked an undergrad student if he can use the hand sanitizer that's hanging off her backpack in some kind of Hello Kitty dispenser. So I'm definitely a little bothered.

But I'm clear-headed enough to recognize that it could have been much, much worse. And so it stands to reason that one of my best friends in the world, who is willingly and gleefully parenting a monkey-creature that is half me, is going to react better than this stranger. That she's going to help me, and nurture me, and support me in every way I need. Telling her will almost certainly be to my benefit.

It's just that it also entails explaining to her why her child can never have a full-blooded sibling. And it also means explaining about my drinking, and everyone from the office, and everything that happened that one night, remembered or not. And maybe, just maybe, it's easier not to have explain any of that at all.

WHAT IT FEELS LIKE TO BE MARRIED

MILES BOARDED THE BUS ALONE.

There was some awkwardness buying his ticket from the driver, who was a man with a wrinkled face and thick glasses that kept catching the sunlight and reflecting it into Miles's eyes.

"Wieliczka," Miles repeated. "Wieliczka." The word was printed on the outside of the bus, but he didn't know how to correctly pronounce it. The driver was nodding and saying things in Polish that Miles didn't understand. Steph was always better at this kind of interaction when they travelled. Eventually he handed over some money in a large denomination, and quietly accepted the ticket and the change that the man handed back. Then they nodded at each other and Miles went to take his seat.

The truth was they'd had a fight that morning. "I have cramps," she'd said. "I'm bloated and tired. You snored half the night." When they had first started living together he would have said, "It's not my fault I snored," but these days he knew better and felt it wasn't worth the effort. She would likely have countered with, "Is it my fault I'm bloated? I didn't choose to menstruate." He would have been tempted to say that she had overly salted her meal the night before and that salt causes water retention, but those were the types of comments she didn't appreciate. He had tried to warn her during the dinner and she'd reacted badly.

"They're cravings," she told him. "Natural cravings to replace the iron and minerals that my body is losing." Since they'd been engaged, she had told him seventeen different times how insensitive he was. He knew it was passive-aggressive to keep count, but he couldn't help it.

They decided she would stay in bed or "find something local to do," and he would go to the Wieliczka salt mine alone. He didn't mind being alone some of the time—really he didn't—but it was no fun for a day trip. Their whole reason for this vacation was to spend time together celebrating their engagement and to scout out honeymoon locations. Kraków was not looking good. Steph found it too grey.

The last time they'd travelled was three years ago, and he remembered it being such fun. Tasks that seemed routine at home were exciting in a foreign country. They would spend an hour buying groceries and have the best time doing it. She would translate the labels on the cans and packets literally, using a guidebook. "This is beast spice," she would say, all seriousness, and he would nod as though it were the most necessary and cherished ingredient.

Now that he was spending the day on his own, he would just buy something overpriced and touristy. His whole day would be like that, which was only okay when you were sharing it with someone. Doing it alone, Miles just felt embarrassed.

If there was nice scenery outside the bus window, Miles missed it, dwelling on the fight. He got off the bus, and a prim Polish woman herded them all inside.

"I recommend you buy any souvenirs now," she said, "as there will not be much time at the end of the tour." Miles hated going to the gift shop first. How could you buy a souvenir to help you remember something you hadn't experienced yet? He looked around, thinking he should pick something up for Steph, but he couldn't decide what to buy. Clothing was too risky because he never correctly guessed her size or which colours she would like. He wanted to get her something made of salt, but they only had necklaces in the shape of a cross, and he wasn't sure she would want that. She wasn't religious.

After the gift shop Miles located the tour guide where she stood waiting for the group. She was standing beside a trough of flowing water, which she explained was an underground estuary. She invited him to taste it. The water was very cold and more strongly salty than he had imagined. He had expected it to taste like brine, or tears, but it was like the ocean, stronger. The group assembled. There were middle-aged couples and a few teenage girls speaking French, and a handful of seniors, including many women and just a couple of men—one was tall and wearing an old-fashioned hat.

"Please follow close behind me and do not stray from the group," the guide said. "These mines are very old and very large, and if you get lost you could wander for many days before someone found you. The way down is steep, so please hold on to the support at all times. If you need to stop for a break, please let me know."

In single file they walked slowly down a narrow stairway that had a smooth wooden railing on one side. There was a constant dripping sound, and the stairs were slippery. But no one fell.

At different spots the guide stopped and pointed out statuary that the miners had sculpted.

"Here we see a depiction of miners," she said. "Here were see the miners have carved the likeness of some saints."

Miles couldn't make anything out. They just looked like stalagmites to him, lumpy protrusions out of the ground. The statues had changed over time, the guide explained—the moisture in the air dissolves the salt and obscures the detail, smoothing ridges, filling declivities, turning everything back into a blob. Miles found it depressing.

After descending for a long time, they came to a giant ballroom carved entirely from salt. It had intricate chandeliers hanging from the ceiling, and the floor looked like polished tile. The walls did too.

"Pope John Paul II said a mass here," the guide informed them.

The salt was dirty. That bothered Miles. He had expected white sparkle and the purity of crystal, like the diamond ring he had bought for Steph. Instead everything was a dull grey. The guide explained that minerals made the salt coloured, and that there were several different colours depending on which specific minerals were in the soil. But they did nothing for him. What good was a cathedral if it was drab?

"Every year, many Polish couples get married in this mine," the guide told them. Miles couldn't imagine it. How could anyone ask a woman to invite her family deep into the earth to give her away in all this gloom?

He knew they were near the end because the guide changed her body language. She was more relaxed, perhaps because she knew it was almost time for her break. She had brought them to a narrow cavern that seemed to have natural light and was several storeys tall.

"Here," she told them, "there is the most wonderful echo." She called out the word once—"Echo!"—as if to demonstrate she wasn't lying, and it dutifully bounced back several times. There were impressed murmurs from the crowd. "It is much better than I can demonstrate," she said. "Maybe there is a singer here?" They each looked at the people on either side of them incredulously—was a secret singer hiding among them? And then, as though on cue, a creaky voice eased out of one of the old men—he had taken off his hat and was holding it against his chest. The guide looked pleased. Miles imagined that not every group yielded a song, but that she felt the best about her tour when they did. A grand finale.

The man sang in a language Miles didn't understand. It went on just long enough to let his mind wander a bit, to think of Steph's face when he'd given her the ring, the way the wind had played with her hair one summer at the beach. He closed his eyes to concentrate on the notes and the melody. There was harmony as the echoes washed back and made a kind of round. And then it was over.

They clapped, and their applause echoed back to them.

The guide beamed and lifted her arm in an ushering sweep, but before she could say anything, the old man who had sung cleared his throat.

"Where's my wife?" he said.

They all looked around again. The women who were close to his age shook their heads and hunched their shoulders in perplexed shrugs.

"I'm sorry, what did you say?" asked the guide.

"My wife," he said. "She missed my song."

It took a moment for the guide to answer. When she did, her accent seemed stronger. "What is her name? When did you last see her?"

Miles couldn't remember if he'd seen the man's wife. With old people, it was so hard to figure out who was with whom. People were huddling into smaller groups and looking miserable. The French teenagers whispered to each other. The guide was talking in Polish on her walkie-talkie.

"Sir, you will have to come over here," she said. "The rest of you, please get onto the elevator. It will be a six-minute ascent to ground level. Please do not panic if you have any claustrophobic feelings."

Miles bundled into the elevator along with the rest of the group. As the elevator went up they heard creaks and groans, and it was completely dark. All he could hear was breathing.

"That poor man," someone said in the darkness. "I hope they find her."

When he got back to the Airbnb apartment they were renting, Steph had made him dinner.

"I tried to make pierogis," she said. "And white borscht."

For a second he was angry because she had done all of it without him, but the soup smelled good and he felt so happy to see her. He supposed they had to do some things separately so that the things they did together would always seem special.

Over the meal he told her about the mine, and when he got to the part about the woman who had gone missing, he was surprised to see Steph was crying.

"That's awful," she said. She spent much of the rest of the night on her tablet, scouring English news sites and social media, looking for an update. She didn't find anything.

In the morning, she was still thinking about it.

"Why don't we go today?" Miles suggested. "We can take the tour together, and we can ask them if that woman is all right."

Steph agreed to go, and so Miles lived the first part of his day over again, except this time Steph was at his side. He knew how much the bus tickets were, and he knew the correct way to pronounce Wieliczka. Everything was better.

When they arrived at the mine, though, it was obvious something was wrong. There were people striding angrily through the parking lot and crowds standing around in groups. Miles went to investigate, then came back to give Steph the bad news.

"I don't understand, are you saying I can't even take the tour?"

"They aren't running any today. They closed down the mine to search for her ... Apparently this is the first time they've closed it since the Second World War."

She looked at him like she was trying to figure out a problem or assess a risk. "I can't believe you brought me here," she said. "This is so depressing."

Steph went to look at the gift shop, and she bought herself one of the salt crosses. Miles didn't say anything. Then they spent some time just sitting on the grass by the parking lot, sometimes talking to other groups of tourists who spoke English. There was one man in a yellow windbreaker, Sven, who Steph kept talking to. Miles thought she was flirting.

Suddenly a man came running out of the gift shop, shouting to his friends. "*Gestorben!*" he shouted. "*Sie is tot!*" Murmurs were passing between all the groups of onlookers in several languages. Sven headed over to where the man was and then came loping back.

Steph looked at Miles, but he didn't say anything. So she turned to Sven and said, "Excuse me, but what did he say? What happened?"

"She is dead," he said, and somehow the cadence of his English made it sound like he was reading a complicated physics formula instead of stating a simple and horrific fact. "They have found she is dead already."

Miles didn't know what to do or say. He glanced at Steph to see how she was reacting.

She brought her hands together and up to her mouth, like she was hiding a smile, or spitting out something that she didn't like.

Her face scrunched a bit and then she fixed it. He could tell she was crying, even though there were no tears.

"She's been dead since yesterday?" Steph asked.

The man looked at her with a kind of pleading in his sky-blue eyes. "You must forgive my English!" he said, as though it were the most the vital matter on earth. He rubbed his hand over his face and through his hair, either collecting himself or flirting.

"She has been a long time already dead," he said. "For a period of many years. This man, they spoke to his daughter. He has ..." Here he pointed at his perfect hair in a gesture that needed no translation. "Problems."

Miles went to ask if they would be reopening. The staff said they were going to be closed for the rest of the day. Many of them had been there all night, and there were still search teams that had to be brought out safely. There was nothing they could do but get back on the bus.

"I have to go to the bathroom," Steph said. "I'll meet you."

When she came and found him in his seat, she snuggled into him.

"There were some women talking in there," she said. He made one of those noncommittal grunts she needed to hear to know that he was listening. "One of them was a neuroscientist, and she was explaining that salt is necessary for memory. It helps the memories get stored in the brain."

"My God," Miles said. "That's ironic." He was never sure if he was using that word correctly, but Steph didn't say anything.

He had his arms around her, and he squeezed a little. After a minute or two, he spoke again. "I can't believe he could forget that his wife died."

"I don't think that's it," Steph said. "It's not that he forgot his wife died. It's that he remembered always having her with him. He just remembered what it feels like to be married. That's how he spent most of his life."

They were quiet after that. During the drive, Steph fell asleep leaning against Miles, resting her head on his shoulder. He could smell her berry shampoo. He tried to keep his breathing very even and steady. He didn't want to wake her.

SWIPE RIGHT FOR CHAD

THE DATE WAS to happen at the castle, the one built by an eccentric old architect who was rich and whimsical enough to put this monstrosity in the middle of the city, such a mixture of styles, such an eyesore, that Europeans came just to scoff at it and deride its very definition as a castle. In the daytime there were tours, but I had never been on one. On the grounds, joggers flitted about like bunnies, and the most aspirational of them ran up and down the towering set of narrow stairs that led down the steep hill to the regular sidewalk and street.

I hadn't been using the app since the guy who left me with bruises. I remember sucking him just so he would leave, my own penis flaccid and cowering between my legs. He was scary, and I learned how dangerous it is to let strange men into your home. But I was still so lonely.

It's only once I saw Chad that I understood why he wanted me to meet him at the Casa Loma stables. I thought maybe he worked there and wanted to head for a drink right after work, keeping it casual, showing me his working-man realness, very butch. It was like this poem I studied in high school English: "The sweat of the working man / stiffens my resolve." But it turned out that he lived there.

The thing to remember with the app was that there were always surprises. This time, it was the four legs, the strong horse body, the massive dick hanging like a bell clapper between his hind legs. His profile hadn't mentioned that he was a centaur.

It's such a strange feeling how, leading up to dates, I'm excited, anticipatory. I can't wait to meet this amazing person I've been dreaming about and making up stories about, fantasizing all the way. Or wondering what their voice will sound like, what my deal breakers are and where I'm going to draw my boundaries. But then when I get there, if the guy is good looking or charming and obviously real and not a flake or a catfish or a jerk, I tend to get awkwardly silent and stiff and then I worry the whole time about not being more natural and how the guy will likely never want to see me again.

Chad was attractive. All his photos were from the waist up, and now I knew why. *Swipe right for Chad* was his entire bio. It made me laugh. And so I swiped.

Getting a match isn't as common as people who have never used apps think. But at the same time, I can't help but wish it were harder. We all want the algorithm to be so smart, so insightful, that it somehow knows only the people who will be our true soulmates, or the people we can really end up with and be happy. We want it to be at least as effective as a matchmaking family elder, but without any of the concomitant guilt or obligation or restriction on lifestyle. We want freedom and to get exactly what we want at the same time. We want to have choices while our partners stay monogamous.

I have a problem with doing too much research when I'm interested in someone new. It's a way to funnel my obsessive mind. Usually it comes through the form of trying to learn another language. I match with a guy who's proudly Portuguese? Out comes the Duolingo and suddenly *Eu faleu um pouco.* When I briefly dated an Anishinaabe artist, I was looking up classes in Ojibwe well before our first date, not to mention marriage traditions.

With Chad, after I learned what he was, I found myself reading everything I could get my hands on about horses. For example, did you know there are four kinds of horse vocalizations? Whinny, nicker, snort, and squeal.

Of course with centaurs, the half with the brain, the half that communicates with language, is the supposed "human" half. Which means all of this research could have been for nothing—insulting or just irrelevant.

As we walked along the pathway beside the hedge, his hooves made loud clopping noises on the flagstones. I tried to figure out if it would be classified as a canter. I tried to count it as a time signature, to figure out how I would score it. It was rhythmical and comforting, and it gave me something to focus on when he was being boring. I could imagine us walking together for whole days. The setting would change—suddenly mountains on the landscape, next a muddy field in springtime, then, because the idea of footprints was in my mind but I couldn't quite imagine what he would wear in cold weather, I imagined us on a beach with big ocean waves crashing in around us.

What surprises me now is that I never even thought about riding him. It's so hard to explain how it felt completely out of the question, not just that I didn't feel comfortable asking but that I didn't want to. If anything, it changed the way I felt about piggyback rides—there's that animal word again, though I'll be damned if I've ever seen a pig carry anything at all, let alone a rider. Why is that we feel entitled to jump on each other and be carted around? Unlike royalty in their litters being carried to and fro, humans are meant to get places on their own two feet.

"Don't you ever feel you should ... put on shorts?" I asked. From the look on his face, I immediately regretted it. He hardened, and darkened, and then an angry little furrow appeared between his eyebrows.

"Why should I hide myself? And why should I have to conform to be more human?"

"It's just ... I keep looking at your dick. I can't help it. And it's not something I have to worry about usually on dates."

"This isn't a usual date." He said it suavely, with a smile, and so we turned it into a chance to kiss. But there was no tongue and it didn't feel like either of us were that into it. Or at least I wasn't, not yet.

When we got back to the stables, a tall and handsome man walked by us, and he and Chad nodded at each other in a way that felt familiar.

Because I'm trying to be more assertive, I asked him whether they had been involved in the past.

"He's the stable boy. I could never be with him," the centaur said. "I mean, he literally shovels my shit."

I thought then of my ex, Jacob, who had died of cancer, and all the times I'd helped him clean himself up after he shit himself from the chemo or the radiation. I thought of my friends with babies and how they were always changing their diapers and carefully wiping their bums. It seemed to me like shit was part of love.

"Well, I guess it's getting pretty late," I said.

I have a friend who, on dates, counts how many times her date asks her a question about herself. It's because she's dated a lot of narcissists (I relate, and I bet you do too), and her therapist advised her to look for red flags of narcissism in this way. "I just want someone who's going to ask me questions about me," she says.

My parents said similar things when my oldest sister finally brought home a guy and told them she was going to get married. He was a lot younger than her, and he didn't know what to say around my parents. He would answer their questions as though he were being interviewed, maybe not by the cops, but by a pernicious cross-examiner at a trial. Everything was factual, precise, unambiguous. And he showed utterly no curiosity about them, their lives, or even my sister's life before she had met him. We all thought it was odd, but just said that we wanted her to be happy no matter what.

That's not something my parents ever said to me, after I told them. I wondered if a centaur would be worse for them, being non-human, or if the fact that I liked men had already made me alien in their eyes. Whether having half a horse's body wouldn't be the part that bothered them about Chad so much as the genitalia between his legs.

"I think you're really brave," my friend tells me. "Connecting with another person is hard enough, but you're trying to make a life with a totally different type of creature. It's going to be hard for you to build a world together, when the worlds you come from are so totally different."

This sounds bad, but she says it with a very positive tone of voice, so I just look down and nod my head.

"Sitting is the new smoking," Chad told me one night, when I was talking about wanting to buy a new lounge chair. "Your species has finally figured it out after all these centuries of chairs. Mine never went much for furniture, of course." When he said something he thought was funny, and I didn't laugh, his breath came out in this skittering sort of lip flubble that was more equine than I think he knew.

We had so many conversations about whether or not I could meet his needs. It was our main topic of conversation. Always whether I would be able to handle him, handle something about his personality, or his nature, handle life with him. We never, ever talked about whether he could handle me, or whether he could meet my needs. It wasn't just that he didn't remember I had them, it was that I forgot I had them too. Which of course, was a big part of why things fell apart.

It struck me as funny, at times, that Jacob never seemed to wonder whether or not I would stay. There was no conversation where he gave me his blessing to move on, or even just to sleep with someone on the side, knowing full well that I would say no, of course not, I don't need that, I don't want that. There was no talk of what would happen to me after he passed. It was as though I was just an extra in the movie of his life. Or not an extra—the supporting character of the supportive boyfriend, with no narrative arc of his own.

It was clear Chad didn't expect me to leave or stray either, but for different reasons. It wasn't that he needed me; he had the stable hands and the other centaurs and his fair share of suitors, I'm sure. And so the tension of our relationship became the inverse of the one I had with Jacob: instead of feeling like I couldn't leave, I became obsessed with why he wanted me to stay. Why me, out of all the possible dudes out there? What was Chad getting out of being with me?

Jacob's chemo was always at Princess Margaret, a name I associate only with cancer now. What a funny way for royalty to be known in modern times: a "Prince Albert" is a piercing in your dick, to "Princess Diana" is to drive your car into a concrete overpass. To "Princess Margaret" became a verb for us, which meant going for treatment and, sometimes, surviving cancer itself.

"When I finish Princess Margareting," he'd say, "I want us to go to Jakarta."

He'd never talked about Jakarta before. I doubt he could have pointed it out on a map. Though I sometimes think I was too judgmental about his intelligence and education.

"We can do that," I'd say, though I had no intention of going. That, and we both knew he was going to die.

The sex was exciting, because it was so new, and so different from everything that had come before. When I stood behind Chad, he would raise his tail, and I could lick his asshole standing up. That was new. To have me suck him, he would have to rear up on his hind legs, his front hooves slamming into the brick wall feet above my head, his massive erection urgently before me. I couldn't even get the head of it in my mouth, not the whole thing. But I stroked him with both hands and licked him all over and he neighed and whickered in delight. Once I put my whole arm inside him. It was more than just sex, and somehow also less. It never felt bestial because he was so verbal, always talking, encouraging me, directing me, commanding me.

What I liked about it was that he was strong. He was healthy. He smelled alive; even the gross notes were of vaguely pleasant things like manure and dirt and loam. He smelled of hay and leaf rot and open fields. His flesh was hard, so hard, with muscles that rippled and jumped beneath my hands. He was warm. I never once saw him shiver, or tremble, or even hesitate. He was such a scion of willpower and strength and beauty and confidence.

Of course those things never come alone. There was arrogance, and cruelty. But I kept going back.

It made me feel safe when I stroked his flank.

I thought that showing up at a hipster party with a centaur would give me some cred. *Look at that guy, he's so cool.* One of my straight married friends said to me once, "Well, you certainly don't seem bound by any traditional societal conventions." The way he said it was like it was supposed to be a compliment, but the kind you think you're supposed to pay someone, when it's the opposite of what you actually think. Or at least, that's how I took it, but I never know if that's just my own paranoia talking.

I was getting dirty looks from the other guys. Or were they interested looks? My friends say that I am way too self-critical, that I self-sabotage by taking everything as an insult before really giving people a chance. There was one guy with a dangling earring that looked like some kind of crystal, and he had a really huge moustache that looked like it was waxed and sculpted. Every time I looked over at him, he seemed to be staring at me.

Chad cantered off without telling me where he was going, and this moustache guy took the opportunity to come over to me.

"Hey, are you with the uh ... the ..." he motioned toward where Chad had been standing. I pretended like I didn't understand, because I wanted to make him say the word. "Oh come on, man ... the uh ... cryptid? Is that what I'm supposed to say?"

"His name is Chad." I hated the way it sounded when it came out, bitchy and whiny instead of pointed and castigating.

"So are you with Chad?" the guy said. The way he was looking at me, I started to wonder if maybe he was hitting on me. He looked amused, and maybe interested. When he twirled his moustache, he looked nervous and flirty rather than like some evil villain, which was kind of hot.

"We're here together," I said. It was as vague and as accurate as I could be. When Chad came back, he saw the guy walking away. His eyes lingered longer than I would have liked.

"What did that guy want?"

I don't know why I told the truth. But I did. "He was asking about you," I said. His smug little smirk burned me.

I found out later that they slept together. I knew I wasn't allowed to be upset about it, and that's what made me even angrier. I was going to pick Chad up at the stables and I saw the guy from the party walking away. Limping away, I should say. Which made me know right away what he'd been up to. Chad lied about it by denying that the guy had ever been there. He could have just told me that the guy had been sleeping with one of the other centaurs, and I would have chosen to believe it. There was no way Chad was the only male one who slept with men, was he?

The lie bothered me for so many reasons. Because it was petty, and small. On the one hand the lie seemed to mean he cared about my feelings, enough to protect them, at least. On the other, I think he knew I didn't believe him, maybe even knew I would have seen the guy on my way in. He had to have timed it like that, so close together. Ultimately, he wanted me to know. But not enough to actually tell me. That communication style felt labyrinthine to me ... not like something that was going to help me build a better future.

I started doing that dance, of wanting to break up with Chad before he broke up with me, but being too scared to actually take any action.

In the end I brought him to see Jacob's grave. I didn't mean for it to be as portentous as it obviously was. I think I wanted to share something about myself, and to let him know that I too felt things he couldn't understand. Like losing a partner, or being mortal at all.

But he just didn't get it. Once he understood where we were, he just said, "It's not me, it's you," and galloped away. The next time I opened the app, he'd blocked and deleted me. I thought about going back to the stables just to try to get some closure, but then I kept putting it off. I'm not sure what I would have said, anyway.

FAR FROM THE TREE

VASHBAIR WAS BORN in the forest, far to the north of the city. He grew up beside his three brothers and under the watchful eye of his mother, but he always felt different from the rest.

Where his brothers took to the normal raccoon interests of expanding their territory, Vashbair couldn't care less; he found trees monotonous and oppressive. While his brothers were always looking for food and working out so they could bulk up and make themselves impressive to females, Vashbair preferred to subsist on only a simple diet of berries and nuts, eating just enough to get by. And most noticeably of all, when they reached maturity, his brothers only cared about the size of their penis bones, and how many females they could mate with in a single day. Vashbair had no interest in the females, which insulted them. There were no other raccoons like Vashbair in the forest, and no one seemed to want to be his friend.

When their mother let them know it was time for them to branch out and find their own territories, his brothers set off together for a den they had heard tell of several kilometres away. They didn't want Vashbair with them, and he wanted to go with them even less.

"Mother," he said one morning as they were washing their paws in the creek, soon after his brothers had left. "Is there something wrong with me?"

"There are no mistakes in nature," she said. "You are exactly as you are meant to be."

"But are you not ashamed of me, that I'm so different from the others?"

"Vashbair, my dear son," his mother said. "From the time you left my body, I have been nothing but proud of you."

She tickled him behind his ears, bringing out the winning smile she saw too rarely on his face.

"If the forest doesn't make you happy, you should leave. Take one final piece of advice from your old mother: Go south, to the city. You will find other raccoons like yourself there, and wonders you could never dream of."

"Won't you miss me?" Vashbair hated the pleading note in his voice.

"I miss all my kits," his mother said. "But that is the way of nature, and there are no mistakes. When you go to the city, you will have expanded our territory farther than any of your brothers, and that will make me proud to think on."

The two of them engaged in affectionate behaviour for a short time, then Vashbair said his goodbyes and set off on the next part of his journey.

And so it was that Vashbair came to the city. The first few weeks were very hard, but in time Vashbair found an apartment in a laneway garage and got a job as a mascot for a small airline that operated from downtown.

For the most part he liked his life of photo shoots and press junkets, walking red carpets and hobnobbing with other mascots and celebrities at private clubs. But sometimes, holding a twenty-four-dollar cocktail and saying the same slogans the marketing team had provided for him over and over, he would think of his brothers in the forest and wonder how they'd fared. And sometimes, watching couples display affection and leave together in Ubers, he felt lonely, and wondered if he ever really would meet another raccoon like him, as his mother had promised.

The other raccoons he did meet were gravely disappointing. Often in a back alley while scrounging for Thai, Chinese, or Indian food—Vashbair found he enjoyed these cuisines, of which there was an abundant supply—he would come across other raccoons. Many were mad with distemper or rabies, some recognized him and hated him for being a sellout to their species, and almost all were vicious and territorial. Only rarely did Vashbair find one who was at all friendly, let alone a male who would want to engage in mating behaviour with him. These encounters brought Vashbair some fleeting pleasure, but the raccoons never wanted to come to his den or even to see him again, and without fail they would set off in search of new territory before dawn broke, never to return.

One day, Vashbair was at a party thrown by the CEO of a new light-rail transit system that was making a bid to build in the city, a project that would span twenty years and cost billions of dollars. The party was the typical sea of blank, uninterested faces, and Vashbair installed himself near a plate of chicken satay skewers and proceeded to eat his feelings of loneliness and existential despair.

And then he saw them: in the corner, standing together, were two raccoons, a male and a female, sipping Veuve Clicquot. Vashbair went over to them straight away.

Raton was a model for the movies—his body was the basis for Rocket in *Guardians of the Galaxy*, one of Vashbair's favourite films, and he spoke with a devastating Québécois accent. Vashbair was so attracted to him that it took all his self-control not to extend his penis bone right then and there at the party.

Raiguma was the most captivating female Vashbair had ever seen, with pale fur and eye rings that extended all the way to her ears. She was a set designer, had been born in Japan, and was travelling throughout North America to find her ancestral village.

"Our kind is considered invasive in Japan," she told him. "The country was importing over two thousand raccoons a year, back in the late seventies and early eighties. It was a pet craze. That's how my ancestors came to Japan, in cages."

When she spoke about it, Vashbair could see the anger in her eyes. "I didn't know about this," he said.

"Sadly, few raccoons over here do," she said. "There are so many of us in Japan now, we've had to occupy almost all of the ancient temples. In some regions they slaughter us, just to keep our numbers down."

Their conversation continued for hours, even as the party wound down around them. After many drinks, feeling uninhibited, Vashbair asked the question he had been desperately running through his mind all night: "Are you two mate-bonded?"

They laughed kindly.

"I only couple with females," Raiguma said. "And Raton prefers males. But we share a den, and we love each other deeply."

That night, Vashbair left in a cab with his new friends. He and Raton engaged in mating behaviour, and afterward they engaged in affectionate behaviour. Raton found the spot behind Vashbair's ears that made him smile, and when they nuzzled and cuddled each other to sleep, Vashbair felt warm and happy.

After many blissful months together, the three raccoons decided that they wanted to raise a litter of kits. They wanted to nurture a family of raccoons who knew the city as home, who would understand interspecies multiculturalism and grow up tasting foods from all over the world.

Raton knew a domesticated and deglanded skunk who belonged to an IVF doctor and knew how to help them with insemination. They decided both Vashbair and Raton would provide semen, and the three of them would raise the kits together.

When Raiguma's belly started to grow, Vashbair could hardly contain his excitement. Not too long ago he had felt condemned to live his life alone, and now he was expecting a litter he would nurture and love along with his lover and their best friend. Each of them rushed home from work now to make alterations to their den in anticipation of the kits. They made a nest of shredded newspaper, and placed Styrofoam lids from takeout containers against the beams of the garage attic to help keep out the cold. They hung mobiles and made rattles from avocado skins and cherry pits. They stored up food so that Raiguma would have enough to eat in the first few weeks when the babies would be blind and unable to hear, before they would be able to take the kits out and teach them to forage.

One night soon after, Vashbair was awoken from his sleep by Raiguma's sounds of distress. The kits were about to be born! Vashbair nuzzled Raton and squeezed his shoulders with his paws.

"Wake up, Raton," he said. "It's time."

Raton and Vashbair went to Raiguma's side. They held her hands and gave her sips of sugar water out of a hummingbird feeder they had stolen. Vashbair thought of his mother and how she had done this very same thing for him and all his brothers. Raiguma struggled valiantly, and she pushed five kits out into the world, three males and two females.

But the babies lay there, unmoving, side by side. Naked and pink and helpless, without fur, they were born still.

None of them stirred. None of them breathed.

The three parents cried themselves to the point of exhaustion. They licked the bodies clean. They memorized each little face, and felt each little body with the most sensitive parts of their paws. Then they tried to decide what to do.

Raton called a bear he knew whose sister had lost a cub; Vashbair called a hotline he had seen advertised on the subway. The hotline told Vashbair his call was important and would be answered in sequence as soon as the next volunteer agent was available. The bear told Raton, "Your whole family should go to see the snowy owl who lives in the abandoned brickworks—she is wise and may be able to comfort you in your grief."

So they wrapped up the bodies of their babies and carried them on their backs. They arrived at the brickworks just after midnight, in the witching hour. They approached the owl, perched white and weightless high above them like a plastic bag stuck on a wire.

"Who, who, who," the owl asked. "Who dares to approach my lair?"

The three raccoons spoke their names.

"Snivelling quadrupeds," the owl said. "Ground sniffers. All day I have laboured at the pharmacy, counting pills and coins, bills and bottles, and interfacing with the world of humans. Though it is not natural for an owl to feel so at night, I am tired beyond words, and my unchecked hunger knows no bounds. Why do you disrupt my solitude?"

"Our litter has been born dead," Vashbair said. "We come to you seeking whatever wisdom you might give us."

The owl swooped down and stood before them, a fearsome bird, larger than they were.

"You may each ask one question," the owl said. "And I will answer it truthfully. But if you would have me ease your minds and give succour to your souls, you must tend to my gnawing stomach. If you will have my wisdom, the price must be paid in flesh."

The three raccoons looked at each other. Desperate, almost mad with their grief, they solemnly nodded their assent.

Raiguma approached the owl first, with two kits in her arms, a boy and a girl. She laid them down before the owl, whose eyes glowed amber like street lights in the night.

"Wise owl," Raiguma said. "What did I do wrong?" She was thinking about a drink she had to celebrate right after they had inseminated, and a cup of caffeinated coffee she snuck at work after a night when cramps had kept her up, and the unpasteurized cheeses and cured sandwich meats the three of them had shared not a week before the birth.

The owl regarded Raiguma coolly. With a duck of her head and a sickening swallow, the owl ate the first kit. Then she grabbed the second kit in her beak and crunched its soft bones down her throat in three gulps.

"Miserable mammal," the owl said. "You have never known what it is to cherish and protect an egg. You grow your babies inside you like tumours. Do you think you are so powerful that you can alter the course of life as it has unfolded for eons? No, woman, you did nothing wrong. In this tragedy, you are blameless. It is your place to suffer, but do not ask why."

The second to approach was Raton. He held two kits in his arms, a girl and a boy. He laid them down before the owl, knowing he would never hold them again.

"Wise owl," Raton said. "What kind of life would my babies have lived?" He was thinking of all the things he would never get to do with them, the first steps he would never see, the intricate joys of discovery he would never know through his children's eyes.

The owl wasted no time dispatching the two kits down her gullet. Raton had to wait as she adjusted her feathers and suppressed a belch.

"The male would have lived a good life," the owl said. "He would have had many kits of his own, and they would have formed a band of family singers that would tour all over the world."

The owl blinked her large, amber eyes. "But the female, she would have caught distemper and wandered into a human backyard. The humans would have called animal control, which would have taken her in a net at the height of her distress, and euthanized her on a stainless-steel table, and incinerated her remains."

Raton took small steps back into the shadows, shaking with tears, and slumped into Raiguma's arms.

It would be the last time she held him.

A few weeks later, Raton and Vashbair will be eating a quiet meal together, and Raiguma will come home to their apartment after having been out for several days. She won't say anything, but they will smell right away that she is pregnant. She will see on their faces that they know, and that the litter isn't theirs, and she will begin to cry.

"I'm so sorry," she will say. "It was instinct. I just couldn't resist it. The urges were so strong."

"It's okay," Raton will coo at her. "It doesn't matter if the babies aren't ours. We can raise them all together anyway." He will look to Vashbair for reassurance, and Vashbair will nod vigorously.

"No," Raiguma will say. "I'm sorry. I am too far from my homeland, and for me this territory holds neither luck nor joy. I am taking my leave of you and returning to Japan to start my family."

After they all cry for a while, Raton and Vashbair will help her pack her bags and take her to the airport. As they watch her plane rise into the sky like a giant white-metal bird, they will hold each other's hands.

Vashbair was the third to approach the owl, the final, smallest kit in his arms, a boy. He placed his son lovingly on the grass before the monstrous bird.

"Wise owl," Vashbair said. "My friends and I are different from our littermates. Each of us has left home and journeyed far from all we knew, in search of something better. This is how we found each other and how we set out to create a family of our own."

"Ask your question," said the owl.

"I shall," Vashbair said. "Is what my mother told me true, that nature makes no mistakes?" He was thinking, for the first time in a long time, of the smell of pine sap after rain, and of his brothers wrestling before a meal. He was thinking of his mother's paws on the spot behind his ears.

The question hung between them in the air. Vashbair could hear Raton and Raiguma taking ragged breaths, he could see the chest of the owl rise and fall, and his own breath whistled in his ears. Only the child was still.

The owl devoured her final prize. She locked her inscrutable gaze on the mournful raccoon before her.

"Yes," she said finally. "Your mother's words are true."

Then she soared back up to her perch, and the night returned to silence.

ACKNOWLEDGMENTS

I gratefully acknowledge the support of the Toronto Arts Council (Writers Level Two) and the Ontario Arts Council (Writers' Works in Progress and Recommender Grants for Writers) for their funding of this project. A special thank you to the juries and recommenders who took a chance on this work; your support is more appreciated than you will ever know.

I sincerely thank the editors who worked with me on these stories while publishing them in journals or anthologies, most especially André Babyn and Noor Naga on "Sixteen Seconds" and Daniel Zomparelli on "In Our Own Image." I received mentorship on this manuscript at the Banff Centre for Arts and Creativity and am grateful to that institution, as well as to Meg Wolitzer, Greg Hollingshead, and Madeleine Thien for their guidance and attention to my work. It is much improved for the time we spent together.

The story "A Complete Index of How Our Family Was Formed" was inspired by "A Complete Index of How Our Family Was Killed" by Matt Bell, which was first published as an excerpt and eventually became part of his novel *How They Were Found*. I thank him for the inspiration.

I wish to express my gratitude to everyone at Arsenal Pulp Press, who have welcomed me so warmly into their family. Thank you especially to publisher Brian Lam, to my editor and friend Catharine Chen, and to Cynara Geissler and Erin Chan, the best publicity team ever. I also want to thank Rebecca Poulin for the incredible cover design, which I hope these stories live up to.

I am the type of writer who is prone to wandering, so I am incredibly grateful to those who gave me a place to stay or hired me to watch their pet while I was working on this book: Sarie Jenkins, Bonnie and Doug Klaassen, Zareen and Lucan, Eileen Davelaar, Norman "PJ" Lemieux, Jon Nehmetallah, and the various people I am doubtlessly forgetting.

This book is all about family and couldn't have come into existence without mine. I want to thank my ancestors, specifically my grandfather Dean Kemper and my great-aunt Constance Munro, whose stories inspired parts of "The Mine Monster of Britannia Beach." I thank my parents, Larry and Michele Trafford, for all of their support, love, and patience. I want to thank my daughter, Sophia, for her inspiration and teachings, and I want to express my deepest gratitude to her "team" in Kelowna: Emma, Heather and Rene, Michael V and Françis. I'm grateful for my brother-in-law, Kyle Nelson, for a unique kind of friendship and love, which extends to the whole rest of his clan as well. And a special thank you to my brother, Thomas, for walking with me through various realities seen and unseen while always making me laugh.

Writing is such a weird thing to do and results in being a weird person with a weird life, so I want to thank the people who continuously choose to live it with me, celebrate my weirdness, and keep talking about writing like it is a worthwhile pursuit. Among them are Linda Besner, Erin Deck, Haley Mlotek, Amy Jones, Andrew F. Sullivan, Curtis Cameron, Laura Trunkey, Jennifer Caloyeras, Brendan Bowles, Mitchell McMahon, Stef Seguin, Trevor Corkum, Zsuzsi Gartner, Alex Leslie, Dan McIlmoyl, Matthew Fox, and Dave McGinn.

And most importantly of all: Thank you, dear reader, for choosing to spend part of your one brief life with this book and its stories.

Photo Credit: Thomas Trafford

MATTHEW J. TRAFFORD earned his MFA in creative writing at the University of British Columbia. He has twice been a finalist for CBC Literary Prizes and has received a Dayne Ogilvie Honour of Distinction from the Writers' Trust of Canada and the Far Horizons Award from *The Malahat Review*. Douglas & McIntyre published his first collection of stories, *The Divinity Gene*, which *Publishers Weekly* described as "shot-through with moments of genuine pathos and even brilliance." Trafford continues to publish stories, as well as write for the screen. He is an avid knitter and fibre artist in his alternate persona of Fairy Godfather Knits.